PLATINUM

DOUBLE PLATINUM

Shelia M. Goss

URBAN BOOKS
http://www.urbanbooks.net

This is a work of fiction. Any references or similarities to actual events, real people, living or dead, or to real locales are intended to give the novel a sense of reality. Any similarity in other names, characters, places, and incidents is entirely coincidental.

URBAN SOUL is published by

Urban Books
1199 Straight Path
West Babylon, NY 11704

ISBN-13: 978-1-59983-057-5
ISBN-10: 1-59983-057-4

First Printing: March 2008

10 9 8 7 6 5 4 3 2 1

Printed in the United States of America

1

SMOOTH OPERATOR

"Parris, I hate to tell you this, but Archie has depleted almost all of your accounts," Mark Beckham, my accountant, informed me nearly two years ago.

That was the peak of my personal and professional downward spiral. The media had a field day with the news of my loss. Now, at thirty-two, I had been singing professionally since I was twenty-one and I had an on-again, off-again love affair with the media. One day they loved you and the next, you're thrown to the wolves.

I've been able to hide from the media that I'm battling with depression. The tabloids would have a field day if they knew Parris Mitchell, media proclaimed R & B diva, took antidepressants. At first it was difficult dealing with Archie Walker, my ex-boyfriend and ex-manager, running away with my assistant Sylvia and my money.

Fortunately Archie didn't have access to all of my accounts or I would be flat broke. During the time we were together, I trusted him and I allowed him access to not only my accounts, but my heart. After he left, I felt depleted in more ways than one. The authorities haven't been able to locate him or his partner in crime.

Archie wasn't all that cute, but it was something about him that drew me to him. With an average height and build, he never stepped out of the house without being immaculately dressed. Silly me, I ignored the rumors of him creeping with some of my backup dancers. I confronted him on numerous occasions about the rumors, but each time he convinced me that people were jealous of my success and our relationship.

He tried to pressure me to marry him on many occasions, but I declined due to my hectic touring schedule. Looking back on it, marriage to Archie never crossed my mind. I was content with the way things were. The tension between us grew with each turned-down proposal. If he wasn't my manager, I probably would have ended the relationship sooner and I wouldn't be going through all of this now.

I found out in the newspaper of Archie and Sylvia's marital bliss. Losing Archie hurt, but I was beyond shocked to learn that Archie and the normally shy, conservatively dressed Sylvia knew each other intimately and had been playing me all along.

The last year of our relationship had some of the best months of sex I had ever experienced. Archie tried some things on me that I never knew existed. I was vulnerable and naïve. He could have asked me to sign over the rights to all of my songs and I would have. Instead he asked if I would give him full control over my accounts. Mark privately confronted me with his concerns. When a man was throwing it on you in the bedroom like Archie, you lose all sense of reasoning.

I agreed to remove the two-signature clause from some of my accounts and things started going downhill.

I wish I had never fired my first manager. Dexter Ringo believed in me from the moment he saw me perform in a high school musical. He kept in contact with me throughout my college years and he gave me my first shot at stardom. I wouldn't be here if he hadn't taken a chance and convinced me to move to Los Angeles a day after I graduated from college. He knew the ins and outs of the record industry and promised to make me a star. He did that and so much more. I owe him a lot. One day I plan to make it up to him.

Archie had me under his spell and I began believing the lies he whispered in my ear about Dexter. I fell for the lies and fired Dexter. Dexter was devastated not because of the money, but because to use his own words, "He's a smooth operator, a snake in disguise. I hope he doesn't end up hurting you." His comments infuriated me and I vowed not to talk to Dexter again. A decision I regretted.

I did my best to ignore the critics, but it's been difficult. After I fired Dexter, I only had one more hit CD. The critics have torn my last couple of albums to pieces. It wouldn't have hurt so much if my fans didn't agree. I cried when I read their messages on my Web site. Only my diehard fans have stood by me. For that I'm grateful, but I feel I failed them all by putting out mediocre stuff. Maybe for a new artist it would have been good; for me, my fans expected so much more.

"Parris, you have one more album left to meet your obligation; but I must warn you. If your next release doesn't do well, we won't be renewing your contract," Nathan Rashid, the vice president over at the urban music division, stated over the phone a few days before I found out about Archie's antics.

"What?" I asked, confused. "I've been with you guys since I started singing. If it wasn't for me, you wouldn't be . . ."

Carmen Grisby, my agent, interrupted, "Nathan, Parris will do her part. You just do yours."

In less than a week, my whole world as I knew it began to crumble around me. First the record company, and then the abandonment I felt when I came home one day to find all of Archie's stuff gone. I was frantic and only my mother and Carmen could calm me down. Carmen was on the first plane back to Los Angeles as soon as she heard what happened.

I retreated into a shell, but with her help, I've been able to get my life back together. I agreed to let Carmen handle my business affairs. After the authorities tried tracking down Archie and Sylvia, to no avail, Carmen tried to convince me that I should not allow it to take over my life.

I listened to her and tried, but failed at first. It's taken me two years to get past the anger, hurt, disappointment, and embarrassment of the whole situation. I think I'm finally ready to get some order back in my life. I'm a spiritual person and at first I didn't want to take antidepressants. After a few months of going back and forth with my doctor about it, the realization that God wouldn't have given doctors the power to heal if it wasn't meant to help people. I succumbed and now admit it was one of the best decisions I've ever made. Although I'm not completely off them yet, the dosage had been reduced.

As I sat on my couch reminiscing about my life and thumbing through the latest issue of *Noir* magazine, I realized I was ready to face the music. It's time for me to get back out there and do what I was born to do—sing. There's one more CD under my contract and I refused to fail the record company, my fans, and most importantly, I couldn't fail myself.

2

NO MORE TEARS

"Why didn't you answer the phone last night?" Carmen Grisby shouted on the other end of the phone. She sounded more like my mother than my best friend and agent.

"There's this reporter who won't leave me alone. No matter how many times I change my number, she finds it and calls me," I responded, feeling upset about the numerous unwanted phone calls.

"Maybe you should think about hiring security." I could hear the concern in her voice.

"Carmen, I'm fine. The anxiety attacks are under control," I reassured her as I pressed the speaker button on the phone.

"You can't keep living like this. First Archie, now a meddlesome reporter." Carmen went on a rant.

"I'm fine. There're no more tears here. How many times do I have to tell you?" I stirred my cappuccino and took a seat in my favorite lime-green chaise chair.

"You'll have to remind me until I hear you say you're ready to sing again." She sighed.

"I'm more than ready." I said it more to convince myself than Carmen.

I could hear Carmen fumbling with something on her end. "In that case dear, we will have you in the studio real soon. I need to make some phone calls and we're back in business."

Sipping on my cappuccino, I responded, "I'll be here."

Carmen whispered, "Parris, are you sure you're ready? It's not like when you started. Nowadays these young women are too busy booty shaking to make good music."

I ran my hands over my body. Just another reminder of how I needed to tone up. "They don't have anything on me. I still look good."

"I don't want you to go back into a depression when the record exec comes to you and says he wants you to dress a certain way."

I was disappointed in her lack of confidence, but didn't let her know it. "I don't have to show my goodies to sell CDs."

"That's my girl. Let me go. I have a lot to do. I'll call you later."

Before I could respond, Carmen had disconnected the call. The annoying sound from the phone interrupted me as I took my last sip. I hit the disconnect button on the base of the phone and poured myself another cup.

"Ouch," I yelled, as I stretched and fitness expert Donna Richardson's voice boomed from my TV screen. I ordered one of her aerobics videos and it came in the mail last week.

It's taken me a whole week to motivate myself into starting a new exercise regiment. I should hire a trainer, but I'm determined to do this on my own. Besides, I didn't want to give the tabloids another reason to paint a fat suit on me and blast it all over the newsstands and Internet with the headlines PARRIS MITCHELL BALLOONED TO TWO HUNDRED AND FIVE POUNDS when I'm a hundred and fifty-five pounds.

"One more," Donna's voice said.

"You can do this," I told myself.

An hour later, I took the monogrammed towel with a big P on it and wiped the sweat from my face and neck. I left my exercise room feeling good. After talking to Carmen, I needed a game plan. The first thing was to get back in shape and increase my stamina. I wanted to do a full-blown publicity tour and I needed the energy.

The kitchen was one of my favorite places in my five-bedroom house. I've redecorated the kitchen twice in the past year. I told myself I would wait another two years before changing things. The canary-yellow tiles on the floor along with the sunflower wallpaper brightened the room.

I ran my hand over the steel counter and wondered if I should have left it alone so it would match the light brown wooden cabinets. I shook my head knowing I did the right thing. I love vibrant colors. Hadn't always, but these past two years have taught me life was too short to be around drab colors. I gave my old dishes to a shelter and bought a slew of multicolored dishes that now graced the inside of the pantry.

As I opened the dishwasher, I realized they weren't

clean. I ran out of dishwasher detergent two days ago. Fortunately I had enough glasses in the house. I hardly ever used the same glass twice. I don't have a live-in maid like some people I know. Missy, my maid, normally came in three times a week. In between time, I kept things neat and in order.

I opened the iron-steel refrigerator, but was disappointed after moving the milk carton and apple, cranberry, and orange juice around. I was out of bottled water and I refused to drink tap water. I took a glass out of the cabinet and poured myself a tall glass of apple juice. It was enough to quench my thirst temporarily. I pulled out the drawer near the stove and picked up a steno pad, which listed items on my grocery list. I added bottled water to the list and tore the sheet off before returning the pad to its rightful place.

Grocery shopping was my least favorite item on my to-do list. I hired Ellen Danielle Personal Shoppers to take care of all of my personal shopping. On occasion, I'll take a trip to the closest discount store. Some people were surprised to see me do my own shopping and at the number one discount store at that. Mama didn't raise a fool. No matter how much money was in my bank account, I refused to pay outrageous prices for things; except when it came to my purses. There's no such thing as too high of a price for a good and stylish handbag.

The funk from my arms made its way to my nostrils. The phone rang, but the first order of business was a hot shower. Whoever was on the phone could wait. The phone never rang when I was sitting around bored. It didn't take me long to walk up the winding stairway to my bedroom. The pink-and-white striped comforter was halfway off my high-post cherrywood bed. In my haste to get my first cup of coffee this morning, I left it unmade. It too would have to wait. I laughed because back in my hometown of Shreveport, Louisiana, my mama wouldn't allow us to leave the room until our beds were made.

With a minimum of a hundred pairs of jeans, the one pair I wanted to wear, I couldn't find. I went through the clothes hanging in a neat row up in my main closet. Each section of the closet was separated. On one side, shirts and blouses hung, on the other side, dresses, skirts, pants and jeans. I had a special section for my shoes and accessories, which included my collection of handbags. After spending way too much time looking for one pair of jeans, I grabbed a pair of black faded ones and a T-shirt off the racks. I threw them on the bed and retrieved a matching pair of purple-laced underwear from my dresser drawer.

With my clothes in one hand and a washcloth and bath towel in the other, I entered my other sanctuary. The huge bathroom, decorated in pink, had gold-trimmed his-and-hers sinks and a sunken whirlpool tub. The shower was in a separate section. Most important to me was the cute little vanity area full of my favorite bath and body products—from bath salt to lotions from Carol's Daughters. Some might find it eccentric, but my bathroom would be incomplete without the midsize plasma TV/radio/CD player in the corner.

I removed the sweat-drenched clothes from my body and threw them in the hamper. Now it was time to do what my body was yelling for me to do earlier, wipe the funk off. The stream of water flowing from the showerhead seemed to wipe away not only the sweat, but also the self-doubt. The rejuvenating flow of the beads of water hitting my body allowed my mind to think of positive things. Of how precious life is. Melodies of songs I had never heard before entered my thoughts. I couldn't wait to get back in the studio. Life was good. There was only one thing missing, a special man to share it with.

The water turned cold, which alerted me it was time to exit the shower. I rubbed Ocean Shea lotion over my legs and arms. I loved the way it felt against my blemish-free, mocha-brown skin. "I smell so sweet I might need to put on a repellent to keep the bees away," I chuckled while dressing.

I decided to take a trip to the store myself instead of waiting on the services of Ellen Danielle. I confirmed that my wallet was in my Dior Logo Saddle handbag and grabbed my keys and cell phone off the cherry-wood dresser. I turned the house alarm on and exited to the garage via the kitchen to get into my custom-painted marbled chameleon pink, late model convert-ible BMW. The sun was out, so I put on my Christian Dior shades and checked my messages while pulling out of the driveway.

"We've chosen you to sing the title track for my next movie soundtrack," I heard Rose Purdue state. She paused and continued, "I've told Carmen and I won't take no for an answer."

Just because Rose won an Academy Award and got her star on Hollywood Boulevard, she felt that she could make demands on everyone. She was more than a hand full. If it wasn't for Carmen, or the fact we were from the same hometown of Shreveport, I probably wouldn't deal with her at all. After the way she dogged her sister, there was no way I would let her anywhere near my man. Well, if I had a man.

To my dismay, I saw flashes when I pulled onto the

street. Without realizing it, I almost hit one of the paparazzi cameramen who had jumped off the curb to get
a closer look at me leaving. I jumped on my brakes,
said a few obscenities after realizing the guy was all
right, and sped away.

Before I could call Carmen, she was calling me. I
didn't give her a chance to talk. "What are these fools
doing outside my house? I bet you Sandy Blair is
behind it."

"Calm down," Carmen responded.

"She needs to get herself some business and stay
out of mine," I yelled.

"That's the price of fame."

"Whatever," I stated, frustrated that my day was
ruined because of some nosy folks who don't know
how to leave me alone. I was about to end the call with
Carmen, when I recalled Rose's message. "And another thing, tell Ms. Purdue, the answer is no."

"Too late. I told Rose you would do it."

I jumped on my brakes. The car behind me blew its
horn. I threw up my middle finger. When the light
turned green, I sped off. I didn't feel like arguing with
Carmen, so I said, "Fine. But next time, check with
me before committing me to something."

I hung up without waiting on Carmen to respond.
There's a thin line between an agent and a friend.

3

YOU LOOK
GOOD TO ME

I spent the next few weeks jotting down the melodies that popped into my head. Only thing missing was a producer. Rose's fiancé, Lance King, was a producer and he and I had worked on quite a few projects before, but I knew working with him on the movie soundtrack would be enough this time around. I wasn't in the mood to deal with Rose and her over the top diva attitude. I didn't want her man. If I did, I could have had him a long time ago.

Carmen mentioned a few other producers, but none of them seemed to have the type of sound I was looking for. It was time for me to do some research of my own. I had no choice but to sit through music videos that left nothing to the imagination and barely had anything to do with the lyrics of the songs.

I spent time in some of the chat rooms online to see

who was hot and who was out. My ego was relieved to see people hadn't forgotten about me. Some chatters went as far as to say they wished Parris would come out with something new and put some of the new singers to shame. If they only knew "songbird," the chat name I used, was actually the R & B diva herself.

The knock on the door jolted me from a trance. I glanced at the clock and realized I had been on the computer for far too long. "I'm coming," I yelled. I turned the computer monitor off and ran to the front door.

After peeking through the curtain, I saw a package delivery truck outside. I opened the door to a young Hispanic guy with the curliest charcoal hair I had ever seen. There's something about a man in uniform. "How are you today, Ms. Mitchell?"

I looked at his name tag and responded, "Fine, Marco."

My libido was in overdrive; it had to be because I was drooling over this guy who looked barely old enough to drink. He handed me an envelope. "Wait. I have something for you," I said as I went in search of my wallet.

He was standing in the doorway looking around when I got back to the door. I handed him a crisp twenty dollar bill. His eyes gleamed. "Thanks, Ms. Mitchell," Marco said before walking away.

Before I could close the door and lock it, I had torn the envelope seal open. Inside was my invitation to the Black Essence Awards for Music or as my colleagues and I call it the BEAM awards. It would be a great time for Carmen to announce that I was coming back with a new CD, and I was sure she'd do her best to get me booked as a presenter.

Due to security measures, if you don't have the invitation or your name isn't on the list, no matter who you are, you will not be allowed entrance. I placed the invite in a safe place, a secret compartment in my library located on the shelves behind my romance novels. The shelves were filled with books from the classics to the latest contemporary authors. I read anything I could get my hands on. Just like the library, my books were organized in alphabetical order. I haven't read every book on the shelves yet, but one day I would.

Sparkie's was crowded and noisy. It was one of the most popular restaurants on the Boulevard during lunch. If Carmen hadn't been waving her manicured nails in the air, I would have been standing in the long waiting line. In Tinseltown everybody was a star or wanted to be a star, so unless you had an appointment or tipped the maître d' with a few extra hundred dollar bills you would not get a seat.

I made my way through the crowd as a few jealous women turned their nose up as their men gawked. I couldn't help it if I still had it going on. The pink Escada pants outfit I wore accented my curves. I put an extra swing in my walk as my size eight, three-and-a-half-inch Manolo Blahnik heels clicked on the golden brown marble floor.

"I'm so glad you could make it," Carmen said as she talked on her phone while we hugged.

A smile swept across my face. "Things never change."

While Carmen continued to talk on the phone, I ordered a club soda with a twist of lime and read over the menu. I normally ordered shrimp scampi, but didn't have the taste for seafood. I opted for a chicken salad. A waiter took our orders. Since Carmen was still talking on the phone, I scanned the room and acknowledged a few people I knew by smiling, nodding my head, or with a slight hand wave.

Carmen wasn't what most people would call beautiful. Don't get me wrong; she's not ugly either. With her immaculate dress from head to toe, bob-cut hairstyle with her signature bangs and radiant smile, she could make the prettiest woman feel insecure.

She had a way about her that demanded attention. She's perfect for this type of business. She worked for one of the big four management firms for five years before branching off on her own. Since then, she has become one of the highest paid and most sought after agent in the entertainment industry. She normally doesn't deal with music artists, but once she agreed to take me on as a client, she realized she needed to branch her services out. I'm so proud of her.

"Sorry dear, but when duty calls."

I interrupted Carmen before she could finish, "I know, it's your job to handle it."

Carmen laughed. "Glad to see you're in a jovial mood today."

"Life is good."

"I need a drink and it's not even one o'clock," Carmen stated after glancing at her black diamond designer watch.

I twirled the straw and took sips of my club soda. "Don't let your work stress you out."

"Easy for you to say." She took out her makeup mirror and used her hand to smooth over her bangs.

"When you die, they're going to bury that mirror with you," I joked.

"We're meeting someone here and I wanted to make sure I looked the part."

I looked up. "I didn't know *we* were meeting anyone."

Carmen snapped the mirror shut before dropping it into her small Gucci handbag. "I didn't want to tell you over the phone."

By now, I was antsy. "You know I don't like surprises."

"Don't worry. This will be a welcome surprise," Carmen stated, as I followed her gaze to a man who looked like a chocolate Adonis.

He was beyond handsome. Dressed in what looked to be a custom-made charcoal-gray, pinstriped suit, he strode over to our table. His stylish shades added mystique to the man. My heart was beating so fast, it felt like it wanted to exit my chest. Before I knew it, Carmen was standing up, shaking hands with the object of my increased heartbeat.

"Casper, I'm so glad you could make it," Carmen said as she turned her attention towards me. "Casper Johnson, this is Parris Mitchell."

Casper extended his hand. I knew he probably thought I was a diva, because it took me a few seconds to respond. When our hands touched, I felt a jolt of electricity through my entire body. From the look on his face, I think he felt it too. I flashed my pearly white teeth. "Nice to meet you."

"The pleasure is all mine." Casper took my hand and kissed the back of it before sitting down.

I wanted to fan myself. His soft luscious lips connecting to my skin sent a chill over my entire body. My imagination took over. I wished those same lips were somewhere else. Thank goodness the waiter came over with another club soda. I needed something to cool me down. When he removed his shades, I was hypnotized by the gleam in his hazel eyes. I could hardly concentrate on what Carmen was saying.

"Parris, I was telling Casper you wanted a new sound. I think you two would work perfectly together."

I mentally tried to register his name. A lightbulb went off. It dawned on me that this was the same Casper who made *People* magazine's most eligible bachelor list for the past few years. He was known in the music business as "CJ—The Hitmaker." This was my first time meeting him face-to-face. With his exotic good looks and constant media attention while on the party circuit, he had gained a playboy reputation; a warning sign for me to keep my hormones and emotions in check.

"Parris," I heard Carmen say my name several times before I responded.

"Yes?" I drank the rest of my soda while trying to avoid eye contact with Casper. I could feel him staring.

"What do you think of my idea?" Carmen asked.

"Uh. Uh," I stuttered. "I'll have to think about it."

Casper, in a smooth sexy voice, said, "I would love the opportunity to work with you."

When I looked into his eyes, I wanted to scream, "You look so good to me," but instead I repeated myself, "I'll think about it."

"What is there to think about? You need a hit record and Casper is available," Carmen didn't hesitate to add.

I don't know why I responded the way I did. I felt like the walls were closing in on me. I knew I had to get out of there or I would make a bigger fool out of myself. Thank goodness, my cell phone rang. "Excuse me," I said while answering my phone.

I pretended it was somebody important. It was only the gardener telling me he would not be in until tomorrow. "Yes, I'll be right there. Sorry to inconvenience you."

I hung the phone up and turned my attention back to

Casper and Carmen. "Casper, thank you for coming." Looking at Carmen, I said, "I'll call you."

"Is everything okay?" Casper asked, sounding concerned.

"Yes. No. It'll be all right." This man was going to think I had a stuttering problem. I reached into my purse to pay for my meal.

Carmen halted me. "I got this."

Before I could get out of my chair, Casper was behind me moving my chair back. "Thank you," was all I managed to say.

I didn't hear him or Carmen say another word, because I rushed out of there. "Excuse me," I had to say several times because the lunch crowd had only gotten thicker as I made my way out the front door. The valet brought my car around. I handed him a tip and sped away. My cell phone rang before I could leave the parking lot. I saw that it was Carmen and let it go to voice mail.

I knew she would be upset at me for running out on her and Casper. She'll get over it. I didn't feel like talking to her anymore today, so I'll return her call tomorrow. She's tripping now, so one more day wouldn't change a thing.

"Girl, he was so fine, he had me stuttering," I said, recounting what happened earlier that day to my best friend, Mason Blue.

Mason stated, "I still can't believe you ran out on him."

I fanned myself with my hand. "It was either that or attack him right there in front of everybody."

Mason and I spent the rest of the time catching up

on what was happening in Shreveport and she wanted the scoop on what was going on in Hollywood.

"You know we're getting big-name stars filming here," Mason stated with pride.

"That's what I hear. It's being called the Hollywood of the South," I responded.

"I'm auditioning for an extra in Martin's new film."

"I hope you get it. You've always been overly dramatic," I teased. Mason and I were childhood friends. While growing up, we both had aspirations of making it big one day. She wanted to be an actress and I wanted to be the next Diana Ross. She ended up getting pregnant our freshman year at Southern University in Baton Rouge and had to move back home. After graduating from college at the age of twenty, I moved to Los Angeles and she stayed behind in Louisiana. Mason put her acting plans on hold, went to school during the day and worked at night to keep a roof over her and my godchild Jericka's head. She was now the head RN at one of the local hospitals.

"With a name like Mason Blue, I was born to be a star," Mason said, with a little sadness coming from her voice.

I spent the rest of our conversation trying to cheer her up. Once I got her talking about Victor, her husband of five years, she forgot all about Hollywood. She was blessed to have such a loving and supportive husband. He treated Jericka as if she were his own daughter and treated Mason like a queen. Mason's life looked all right from this point of view. In fact, it looked much better than mine if you took away the glitz and glamour that surrounded me.

4

HEARD IT THROUGH
THE GRAPEVINE

"We heard you were going back into the studio," the stranger's voice said, when I answered the phone after being interrupted from finding out who the killer was in the book I was reading.

It took me a few seconds to register this was an annoying reporter. "No comment," I said and then slammed the phone down.

"Not again," I yelled before reaching for the phone. I checked the caller ID and wasn't familiar with the number. I answered on the fifth ring. "What!"

An unfamiliar male voice came across the other end and said, "May I speak to Parris?"

"It depends," I responded, still annoyed at the reporter's call a few minutes before.

Whoever this man was, he had a sexy laugh. "Depends on what?" he asked.

"If you're somebody I *want* to talk to." I put my book-mark in the book I was reading and laid it on the bed.

"The way you ran out of the restaurant, I'm not so sure."

A twinge of guilt swept my conscience. With his last statement, his voice registered. "I had an emergency." There was a slight pause, so I continued to lie. "Things are okay now."

"Cool," was Casper's only reply.

I felt like a kid who got caught cheating on a test. To change the subject, I asked him a question, although I already knew the answer. "How did you get my home number? I don't remember giving it to you."

"We *both* know it was Carmen." He didn't hesitate to say.

"I don't like people I didn't give my number to calling me."

In Carmen's defense, Casper stated, "She called you several times. An according to her, she only got your voice mail."

I should have hung up but his voice was as demanding on the phone as his physical appearance was in person. "Really, I hadn't had a chance to check my messages."

"Now that we have that straight, I need to know when will be a good time to get together and discuss some ideas I have for your CD?"

I sat straight up in the bed. "I didn't agree to anything."

"But Carmen did."

"Forget what Carmen said. I have the final say so." I slammed down the phone.

The phone rang seconds later. I answered, "What?"

"Did we meet in another lifetime or something? I

swear you act like I stole something from you," Casper said.

I had to hand it to him, he was persistent. "I don't know you. But what I do know of you, I don't particularly like."

"I could say the same about you," Casper responded.

He had me riled up by now. Curiosity had me wondering why he was snapping at me. "I don't think so," I said.

"I heard it through the grapevine that you were a real *diva*," he said in a sarcastic tone.

"Oh really, well this *diva* has better things to do than talk to a man who thinks women should just fall at his feet just because he's . . ." Casper's laughter stopped me from completing my sentence. I hung up without saying another word. Why am I letting this man get under my skin?

The phone rang again, but this time I didn't answer it. A part of me was amused that Casper insisted on talking to me after I hung on him not once, but twice.

I fell asleep with Casper on my mind. He entered my dreams and the only thing that saved me from his wrath was the alarm clock. The book I was reading last night was crushed under my body. I got up and threw the covers off the bed. My bladder insisted on some relief. The bathroom was my first destination. Warm water soaked the lime washcloth. I squeezed it and washed my face. I rubbed cleansing cream on my cheeks, forehead and chin. After making sure my entire face was covered, I plugged in my electric toothbrush and brushed my teeth to rid myself of dragon breath.

Once I wiped the cream from my face, I put on

my workout clothes and headed to my designated gym area in my home. I placed a CD in the stereo. I would ride the bike until it stopped playing. The exercise bike wouldn't work for some reason. I made a mental note to call a repairman. Time went by fast. I had been walking on the treadmill for over an hour when the CD stopped playing and I had worked up a nice sweat.

During the time on the treadmill, I didn't think about Casper once. Well, I did, but it was brief. Before heading to the shower, I swung by the kitchen and took out a forty-eight ounce bottle of water. I had drunk half of it before getting in the shower. The stream of water flowed down my body and for fifteen minutes, I forgot about everything. Since I had no plans of leaving the house, I decided to wear something comfortable. After layering my body with Calvin Klein Escada lotion and perfume, I slipped on a floral shirtdress.

The cord to my laptop was tangled and it took me a few minutes to get situated. I logged on to the Internet and looked up the manufacturer of my exercise bike. I jotted down the number and made a phone call.

"Can you have someone come out today?" I asked the friendly salesclerk. I checked my e-mail while I waited for the clerk to return to the phone. I had tons of spam mail. I hit the delete button. Satisfied that I didn't have any other e-mail that needed my attention, I turned the computer off.

"Hello!" I yelled in the phone thinking the clerk forgot I was on the phone. After a few more minutes, someone finally came back on.

Annoyed, I said, "I was beginning to wonder if you had forgotten about me."

The clerk responded, "Is two o'clock too late?"

"No, that's perfect. My address is 1525 Swan Way."

"Ms. Mitchell, we'll have someone there by two."

We hung up. Next on my agenda was returning Carmen's call. I owed her a good chewing out. As far as I was concerned, we were back to square one and needed to find a producer and fast. I wanted to get in the studio while the creative juices were flowing. Carmen must have been sitting by the phone because she answered on the first ring. She ignored formalities and got straight to the point. "Why did you walk out on me yesterday?"

I was supposed to be going off on her, not the other way around. "I told you I had to take care of something."

"I know you better than anyone. What's really going on in that head of yours?"

"Nothing," I lied. "Everything's all good."

"I'll drop it for now." Carmen sounded annoyed, but I didn't care. She continued to ask, "Did Casper call you?"

"Yes, and don't ever give out my home number without my consent. I might have to change my number."

Carmen laughed. It infuriated me. I asked, "What's so funny?"

"You. He's gotten under your skin hasn't he?"

"I don't know what you're talking about!" I snapped.

"It's about time," Carmen stated in between laughing.

"Look, I didn't call you to talk about what's his name. We need to find me a *producer*."

"I found you one—*Casper*."

"He's not going to work."

"He's the best."

"In whose eyes?" I asked, barely above a whisper.

"According to *Billboard,* his Grammies and other awards," Carmen snapped back.

It's hard to argue with her on that fact. He had at least ten songs in the top twenty. "Well, he's too hip-hoppish for me. I need someone who can produce a *real* R & B track."

"Listen to yourself. This has nothing to do with his music. You know as well as I do that he is more than capable of doing the job."

"Music is the *only* thing on my mind at this point."

I heard Carmen's other line click. "Hold on," she said.

While she had me on hold, I had to think of a way out of working with Casper. It was hard for me to admit that I was attracted to him. I didn't want to be like those young women who were probably at his beck and call. I was too old for it; after Archie, I didn't need a repeat of a broken heart. Warning signals were buzzing in my head to avoid Casper, but it seemed like the music business would bring us together.

"Parris!" Carmen yelled into the phone a few times breaking my concentration.

"I'm here."

"That was Casper. He told me he had to go out of town, but will be back at the end of the week. He wants to get together with you when he comes back so you two can start working on your CD."

Defeated, I asked, "I don't have a choice do I?"

"Not if you want to revive your career sweetie," Carmen said in her sweetest voice.

"I'll call him."

Carmen sounded relieved. "I'll e-mail you his

contact info." Her other line clicked again. "That's the call I've been waiting for. Got to go."

Carmen had disconnected the call before I could respond. Typical Carmen. Why did I feel like I had been railroaded? I had to get a grip on myself. The only thing that mattered now was making a comeback.

5

CALL ME

I spent the remainder of the week exercising, working on my lyrics, and making sure I got enough sleep. I played around on the piano to see if I could notate some of the melodies that were swimming around in my head. Whenever Casper did call me, I wanted to be ready to get it over with. The sooner I allowed him to work the magic he's famous for doing, the sooner we would be able to go our separate ways.

My voice tried to find the right octave as I sang, "My heart is singing a sad song . . . My heart is wondering what is going on . . . Every time I think I've found the one for me . . . Something reveals itself and leaves me feeling lonely . . ."

I couldn't think of the other lyrics right now, so I decided to leave it alone. One thing I've learned since writing some of my own songs is when the creative muse is working, let it flow. When it's not, I can't force it.

This was the ideal time for me to take a jog on the

beach. By the time I found batteries for my MP3 player, the jog didn't seem like a good idea. I opted to lounge near the pool instead. The smell of chlorine floated in the air from the recently cleaned, oval-shaped pool. The sun beamed and the heat radiated, prompting me to remove my jogging suit and discard it on the other patio chair.

Thank goodness my purple matching underwear also looked like a swimsuit. My backyard provided enough privacy where, even if I went completely naked, no one could see me. I felt too lazy to get up out of the chair and go back into the house and pick up a good book. I put my headphones on, leaned back in the chair and closed my eyes. One moment I was singing along with Sade, and the next thing I remember hearing were the sounds of birds chirping as I woke up from a peaceful nap.

I stretched and yawned. "I need to relax out here more often."

Feeling rejuvenated, I picked up the jogging clothes I had discarded and went back into the house. The ringing of the doorbell caught me off guard. "Now who could that be?"

I jogged to the door and peeped through the hole. Casper Johnson stood on the other side. I looked through the peephole twice as if my eyes were playing tricks on me. Before I could respond, he knocked a few times.

"Coming," I called out, as I pulled the shirt over my head and then put on the jogging pants.

I looked in the mirror to make sure no stray hairs from my ponytail and bangs stuck out. I took a few deep breaths and opened the door. "You should've saved yourself a trip and called," I stated while standing in the middle of the doorway.

He towered over me by about five or six inches, so he had to be over six feet. "Since you hung up on me the last time we talked, I figured I would do better by dropping by," Casper said, while smiling and holding a bouquet of yellow and pink tulips.

I stared and didn't immediately respond. He handed me the flowers. My attitude softened. "Thank you. These are my favorite."

"Are you going to let me in?" He leaned against the inside of the door looking as sexy as I remembered him.

"Sure. I'm sorry," I stuttered. I became self-conscious of my attire. "I wasn't expecting anyone."

"You look perfect to me." He licked his lips before walking across the threshold.

"Let me put these up. I also need to change." My knees felt like jelly.

"Don't change on my account," he said.

"I'll be back. You can have a seat in there." I pointed toward the living room.

I left him standing there as I walked up the stairs. I could feel his eyes on me. When I reached the top of the stairway, I turned around. He was caught staring, but he didn't shy away. He smiled before walking toward the living room.

"I need to get a grip," I whispered to myself once behind the safety of my bedroom door. I concentrated on putting the tulips in the empty vase on my nightstand. Once I cut the stems and ran some water, they made a beautiful arrangement. I placed them by my bed. I opened the blinds so they could get more sunlight. By morning, they would have fully blossomed.

I decided at the last minute to keep on my jogging

suit. I convinced myself Casper wasn't anyone I needed to impress. When I reached the end of the stairway I'd changed my mind. I wished I had changed clothes. I stood in the entryway to the living room for a minute watching him. He stood by the mantle looking at my pictures. There was no denying the sex appeal he possessed. For the life of me, I couldn't figure out why he was getting under my skin and we've only met a few times.

Without turning around, he commented, "I was admiring your pictures and awards." He placed the picture down and walked toward me, but stopped and sat on my lime-green couch.

Whew. I commanded my feet to move. Instead of sitting next to him, I fluffed up the matching green floral pillow and sat in the love seat.

We were playing the silent game. Funny thing about it, neither one of us made an attempt to start a conversation. He stared at me and I stared back. I wanted to wipe the smirk off his face. The sound of the phone broke our trance.

"Excuse me," I said before getting up. I turned my back to him when I answered the phone. There wasn't anyone else on the other end, so I hung up. "I guess it was the wrong number," I stated.

"I hate when that happens," Casper said, without taking his eyes off me.

My mind worked overtime as I attempted to retain my balance while walking back to my seat. I needed to gain some control of the situation. "Casper, I know you're a busy man, so I'll get straight to the point."

"My schedule is wide open."

"Then you shouldn't have any problems with me wanting to hurry up and get this project over with." I leaned back in the chair while crossing my arms.

"None at all. In fact, I was going to suggest the same thing." He leaned back on the sofa and threw his left ankle over his right leg.

He's getting a little too comfortable in here. I unfolded my arms. "At least we're on the same page."

"Exactly," he responded.

Was he playing a game with me? I tried to figure out whether or not I should respond to his obvious flirtations. Was my mind playing tricks on me? This man meets beautiful women all of the time. "How soon do you want to start?" I asked, hoping I didn't sound nervous.

"We can start as soon as next week. I've been out of town and once I tie up some loose ends, I'm all yours." He emphasized "yours" a little too long for comfort. I squirmed in my seat.

"Perfect. I'm sure you're a busy man, so I don't want to hold you." I stood.

"Oh you're not."

"I'm sure you're tired from your trip," I stated.

He stretched and didn't move from his seat. "Actually, I'm refreshed. I got here late last night and slept most of the day."

"I don't mean to be rude, but I have some things I *need* to take care of myself this evening." The expression on my face changed to irritation and only then did he decide to get up.

"In that case, I'll leave." He stood and as we walked toward the door, he commented, "I do want to get together before next week. I want to know who the real Parris is; not the one I've read about or seen on TV."

"How about Monday?" I blurted out when we reached the front door.

"Sunday is better for me." He turned and stared deep into my eyes.

He had me under his spell, "Sunday it is," I replied.

He opened the door, but before leaving, he turned around and said, "I'll call you and let you know what time. On second thought, since you're a busy lady, I'll wait for you to call me."

With his last comment, he walked away. I watched him get into his black, chromed-out SUV. He waved before pulling out of the driveway.

6

IF ONLY YOU KNEW

Sandy, the annoying reporter, felt a need to camp outside my property. I tried getting the police to do something, but she would only leave and come right back. According to my attorney, there wasn't anything I could do about it unless I wanted to file stalking charges. A part of me did, but then it would only excite other paparazzi-styled reporters and I wouldn't get a moment of peace.

For the next few days, I blocked out the paparazzi and mentally prepared myself for my outing with Casper. I convinced myself it was not a date but strictly business; however, this analogy didn't stop me from fantasizing about the two of us in compromising situations.

This morning, while in the shower, another stanza for a song crept into my head. I hummed the lyrics. "My mind is telling me to leave you alone . . . My mind's so confused, can't tell right from wrong . . . But every time I think about leaving you alone . . . Something pulls me back into your arms."

I couldn't get out of the shower fast enough. I picked up the notepad by my bed and quickly wrote the lyrics down. Before I knew it, I had also written down a few more stanzas. This was going to be a hit. I could feel it. My phone rang before I could get dressed.

"Good morning," Casper said in a husky voice.

"I was going to call," I lied.

"I couldn't wait a minute longer." He flirted.

A part of me wanted to stretch out across the bed and hold a long conversation, but after hearing the clock chime, I was brought back to my senses. "Casper, pick me up at six. I hate to rush, but I'm running late for church."

"Six it is. Say a prayer for me too," he said before ending the call.

I held the phone for a few seconds before hanging up. My day was off to a good start. I rummaged through my closet and chose a two-piece tan Valentino suit with matching tan three-inch pumps. My jewelry box overflowed with gold, silver, diamonds, and pearl accessories. After a few minutes, I decided to wear a string of pearls necklace. I snapped on the matching pearl earrings. After doing another check in the mirror and grabbing my tan Coach purse, I was ready. I picked my Bible up from off my nightstand and headed to church.

Church service was shorter than normal. The pastor's message hit close to home. He spoke about forgiveness and that was definitely something I struggled with. I could testify how forgiving a person was more for yourself than the next person. I can't say I would forget what

Archie did, but I knew I had to forgive him. I almost drove myself crazy because of the contempt I had in my heart for him. Besides, one day he'll get what's coming to him and I won't have to lift a finger.

"Hey girl, I didn't see you before service started," Carmen said, before giving me a hug.

"I ran a little late," I admitted.

"Do you want to follow me to Roscoe's?" Carmen asked, as we walked down the stairway.

I looked at the time. "No. I'll pass. I'm meeting Casper later for dinner."

Carmen stopped in midstep. "Oh really. I thought he wasn't coming back until next week."

I pulled out my shades and put them on. "He came back a few days ago."

"And why am I just now hearing about this?" she asked, with her hands on her hips.

People started to stare. "Carmen, it's not that serious."

We continued to walk toward the parking lot. Carmen lowered her voice. "I need a contract signed before you go into the studio."

I assured her by saying, "We're trying to get to know each other a little before being cooped up in the studio for the next few months."

"Don't agree to anything without my consent."

We reached her car first. I hugged her. "It's only dinner."

She fumbled for her keys and said, "Make sure that's all it is."

"Carmen, we're not even off the church grounds and your mind is in the gutter."

"No dear, your mind is, because I didn't go there." She chuckled.

"Don't worry. I'm not looking for another relationship," I responded, before sashaying away toward my car.

Carmen yelled out, "Call me when you get in your car."

"There's nothing else to talk about," I yelled back without turning around.

People were looking. I waved at a few people I knew but continued walking to my car.

I decided to return Carmen's call when I got home. If not, I'm sure she would have blown up my cell phone and home phone for the remainder of the day. It's a trip having your agent as your friend. One minute we're talking business and the next she wants to know details about my personal life. Besides Mason, I don't have any sisters, so I'll get over her nosiness.

I began leaving Carmen a message, but before I could finish, my line clicked. I checked the caller ID and it was Carmen. I clicked over. "I was just leaving you a message."

"I had the music up loud and didn't hear the phone until the last ring."

"So what else did you want to talk about?" I figured to cut straight to the chase, because I knew if I didn't, she would.

"Parris, I want details. How did this date come about?"

"It's not a date."

"Sounds like a date to me." Carmen went on and on.

I cradled the phone between my shoulder and ear and poured a glass of lemonade. She was still talking when I sat down in front of the TV. I grabbed the remote and flipped stations. I landed on a music video channel.

"Carmen, one last time, it's nothing. He wants to know more about me, so he can work on the music. That's it."

"If it's nothing, why are you on the defensive?"

I started to say, "If only you knew," but instead I said, "I need to rest before Casper gets here. Call you later. Smooches." I hung up the phone.

My attention was drawn to the screen. Ivan, the male host of a popular video show, profiled Casper right before zooming in and showing Casper sitting in a chair across from him as they discussed some of Casper's upcoming projects.

"What can the industry expect from you next?" Ivan asked.

Casper looked at Ivan and then into the camera, "My next project is one of the biggest highlights of my career. I never thought in a million years I would get this opportunity."

"Sounds good. Can you tell us with who?"

"Right now, I'll like to keep it under wraps. All I can say man, it's going to be the best work I've ever done."

"Ladies and gentleman, you heard it here first. We'll be right back with a video from one of Casper's productions. Thanks Casper. Good luck with your next project."

The interview ended and went to a commercial. I used the remote and turned the TV off. It was good to hear the excitement in his voice concerning our project. I knew at that moment, I had to erase any of the romantic ideas that popped into my head. Our association was strictly business.

7

CONFESSIONS

"You look great," Casper said, as he admired me from the doorway in my black one-piece, knee-length fitted Versace dress accented with black accessories.

"You too," I responded.

He wore a black pinstriped custom-made suit. We hadn't discussed where we were going, but it's clear we both planned on looking good. Without thinking, I reached out to hug him and his embrace tightened and I could feel the soothing rhythm of his heartbeat. I pulled away and cleared my throat. "Let me get my keys and purse."

He dropped his arms to his side. He remained standing in the doorway until I returned. "Let me set the alarm and I'll meet you outside," I said.

Once the alarm was set, I met Casper outside. He stood beside an olive-green Jaguar. Like a gentleman, he opened my door first. "Thank you," I said as he closed the door.

While he walked around, it gave me the opportunity to gather my composure.

"Where would you like to go?" he asked, once behind the wheel.

I smiled and said, "I'm going to be adventurous. I'll let you pick the place."

He looked at me with those big brown eyes. "You sure?"

"Positive." I put on my seatbelt as he pulled out of the driveway.

I looked in the right outside mirror. I thought I saw a car pull up behind us. When I looked again, the car wasn't there. I was curious as to where he was taking me, but refrained from asking. I watched how he made sure to stay within the speed limit as we cruised up I-5. I enjoyed his music selection. "Casper, I'm really digging this CD."

He clicked a button on the steering wheel which turned the volume down. "It's a new artist. It should hit the stores next week."

"He has a great voice."

"My sentiments exactly. Once I heard him, I knew I had to work with him." He mumbled something and it sounded as if he said, "The same thing I said about you."

"I'm sorry I didn't hear you." I used my hands to motion that the music was still a little too loud.

"It was nothing." He changed the CD, this time it was instrumental.

I began singing some of the lyrics I had written earlier. "My heart is singing a sad sad song . . . My heart is wondering what is going on . . . Every time I think that I found the one for me . . . Something reveals itself and leaves me feeling *oh so* lonely . . ."

"Your voice can bring a man to his knees," he interrupted after I hit that last note.

"Glad to hear you like it."

"I can't wait to get in the studio. Your lyrics were made for my music."

His comment brought a smile to my face. We rode the rest of the way in silence as the music played in the background. I relaxed in my seat and enjoyed the ride and the company. I hadn't realized I had dozed off until I felt a light tap on arm.

"We're here sleepyhead," Casper said, as I saw him remove his seatbelt.

I responded, "I'm so embarrassed."

"Don't be." He reassured me by saying, "That means you're comfortable around me."

I laughed. "I wouldn't say all that."

He got out and walked around to open my door. Well, I thought it was him, but when the door opened, the valet had his hand outstretched to help me out. His vest and the outside marquee read L'Orangerie. Casper had chosen a restaurant in West Hollywood. After tipping the valet, Casper placed his arm around my shoulder. We appeared to be a happy couple as we proceeded up the walkway into the restaurant.

The maître d' confirmed our reservations. As we walked to our table, I could feel the love in the air as couples laughed and talked. We were seated in a table in a secluded area of the restaurant. Under normal circumstances, I would appreciate the romantic setting of low lighting, candles, and beautiful floral arrangements on the tables. We were seated and a few seconds later a waitress, dressed in a black tuxedo-styled outfit, came over to the table and handed us two menus.

"Can I get you a bottle of wine tonight sir?" she addressed Casper.

"I would like a sample of your best dry white Bordeaux wine before deciding." Casper looked at me and continued to say, "If the lady likes it, we'll have the entire bottle."

"Yes sir. I'll be right back."

Casper didn't say much. If I didn't know better, I would have thought he was shy. I skimmed the menu but couldn't concentrate. The waitress returned. "Hope this is to your satisfaction," the waitress said, after pouring the wine into a fluted glass.

Casper watched me as I took a sip. "I would like another glass," I said after a few more sips.

After pouring us both glasses, the waitress asked, "Would you like an appetizer before ordering?"

Casper looked at me and asked, "Parris?"

"No, I'm ready to order," I responded. The sooner we ate the sooner we could each go our separate ways.

I buried my head in the menu. I peeped over the rim of the menu and saw Casper looking at the waitress. He said, "Give us a few minutes. I haven't decided what I want yet."

From behind the menu, I said, "The pasta with shellfish sounds appetizing."

"I'm thinking about the roast duck."

"Have you eaten here before?" I wanted to know, because this didn't seem like his type of place. I pulled the menu down and placed it on the table.

"I come here on occasion. Not often enough though."

He was making me nervous. I picked up my flute and drank the rest of the wine. Before I could set it down, a waitress was at our table. "Would you like a refill?"

"Sure." I smiled.

After the waitress walked away, I looked at Casper and said, "That was quick."

"Service here is excellent and expedient."

We laughed. We looked at each other and smiled when the waitress returned to the table and asked, "Are you ready to order?"

Casper motioned for me to go first. I said, "I would like the pasta with shellfish."

"What kind of sauce?"

I looked at the menu before responding. "I'll try the lemon-ginger sauce."

"Excellent choice, ma'am. Would you like a salad?" she asked, as she wrote down my order.

"The house salad would be fine. With lite dressing please."

She wrote down the rest of my order before taking my menu. "And you, sir?"

"The roasted duck served with the wild cherry sauce."

"Rice or potatoes, sir?"

"Roasted potatoes will do. I'll also have the house salad, but with your regular dressing," Casper added as he handed the waitress his menu.

"Someone will bring your salad shortly."

I took another sip of wine. If I didn't watch it, I would be drunk. I hadn't eaten anything and drinking on an empty stomach wasn't advisable.

"Parris, I have a confession to make."

Without looking at him, I said nonchalantly, "If you need to talk I'm all ears."

He reached over and touched my available hand. When I looked up, his eyes spoke volumes. It startled me to see the sparkle in his eyes. "I've wanted to go out with you for quite some time."

I responded, "We just met a few weeks ago."

"We actually met three years ago at a party in the Heights. You were the guest of honor."

"I'm sorry, but I don't recall ever meeting you."

"I didn't expect you to." He sounded dejected.

"Why didn't you try to reach me afterward?" I asked. I knew there was no way I would have forgotten meeting him. He had to be mistaken.

"You were involved with someone else so I didn't feel it was right."

"I don't know what to say. You've caught me off guard." The palm of my hand was sweating. I put my free hand under the table.

He rubbed the top of my hand. "I didn't tell you this to make you sad."

Looking into his eyes comforted me. "I'm fine. It was a long time ago." I removed my hand and giggled.

"What's so funny?" he asked with a confused look on his face.

"Back then I was so into Archie, I wouldn't have responded to any of your advances. During that time my world revolved around that man. My career and my personal life suffered because of it. Boy was I a fool."

"A fool you're not." He sounded reassuring.

"You don't know the whole story," I said.

He looked away. I knew he had heard the stories. I continued to say, "The tabloids had a field day with my personal tragedy. I couldn't walk out of the house without cameras flashing when the story broke."

"The media can be a pest," he interjected.

"Ironically, I should thank Archie for teaching me how to love myself again."

Casper asked, "Did the police every catch him?"

"No, but he and my assistant weren't as smart as they thought they were."

Before I could elaborate on my last statement, our salads were brought over.

I continued to tell him about what happened with Archie and Sylvia. I could tell he didn't expect my candidness. Something about Casper had me confessing things only my mom, Mason, and Carmen knew about the situation. A sense of relief swept over me as I told him everything. By the time our meals were brought over, we were talking like old friends.

"Enough about my past. I'm over it. Tell me about you," I said, after monopolizing the conversation for fifteen minutes or more.

"Not much to tell. I grew up in Atlanta. I have two sisters and one brother. My parents are both deceased."

"Sorry to hear that."

"It's been a few years. I'm just grateful they got to see me succeed."

"Me too." I gave him a comforting smile.

"Where was I?" he asked, quickly changing the subject. "After high school, I became a part of the human beatbox at Southern in Baton Rouge."

"Oh, I know about SU. I was a dancing doll."

"I should have known. You're from Louisiana aren't you?"

"Born and raised in Shreveport, three hours east of Dallas, Texas."

"I had some homeboys from Shreveport."

"It's truly a small world."

"Too bad we didn't meet back then, because there's no way I would have let you get away." Casper flirted.

He was really pumping up my ego. "I graduated early and was long gone by the time you were there."

"You can't be but a few years older than me, if that," Casper said.

I asked, "How old are you and I'll let you know?"

"I'm twenty-seven," he responded.

I shook my head and laughed. "You're a young buck."

"The younger the better. Right?" He winked.

"I hate to be the bearer of bad news, but there's a five-year age gap between us."

"Age ain't nothing but a number. If you wouldn't have told me, I never would have known."

"You're really trying to stay on my good side."

"I'm speaking the truth. You look good."

Twirling my pasta on the fork, I decided to dig deeper and said, "So you only want to get with me because I look good."

"I'm not that shallow. I honestly hope you don't think that low of me," Casper responded.

"A woman can never be too sure these days. If it's not looks or money, then what is it?"

"Parris, let's get some things straight, because I see where this conversation is headed." I wanted to crawl under the table, but I listened.

Casper looked me directly in the eyes and said, "I don't want your money; I have my own. I'll admit I'm very attracted to you, but you have more to offer a man than your looks and your finances."

Looking down at my plate, I said, "I didn't mean to offend you, but you have to understand. I've heard the rumors."

Casper interrupted me, "You of all people should know not to believe everything you hear."

"What about the women?"

"I love women and I'm not going to deny that fact."

"So the papers were right?"

"You didn't let me finish. When I first started in this business, I let the money and fame get to me. I over-indulged in my share of women and parties, but the media always exaggerated situations."

I couldn't believe he was halfway admitting to the rumors. I tapped my fingers on the table, but remained quiet. "That was then. This is now. I'm more selective about who I let into my personal space," he said.

"So you're saying you grew up?" I asked.

"Exactly."

"You didn't have to explain yourself," I said, while taking a sip of my drink.

"And have you wonder about the rumors? I don't think so." He flashed his signature golden-boy smile.

I stated, "I believe only half of what I read, the other half is fabricated."

"Trying to figure out which half is the hard part," Casper added.

We continued to eat dinner. Out of the blue, Casper said, "You might deny it now, but I know you feel something. Don't fight it."

I wanted to slap that confident smirk off his face. I refused to let him get under my skin. "The only thing I feel like doing now is going home."

Casper shook his head. "Tsk. Tsk. Don't deny the truth."

"I only want one thing from you, Casper, and that's a hit record." I picked up my flute and downed the rest of my wine.

"Let's enjoy the rest of our dinner. We have plenty of time to pursue this." He picked up his fork and took a bite of his duck.

"There's nothing to pursue."

He looked up at me, winked and continued to eat. We ate the rest of our dinner in silence. The only sounds I heard were the clinking of our silverware as it touched the plates, and the voices of other patrons.

8

BROWN SUGAR

Dinner couldn't end soon enough for me. After he tipped the valet a second time, we got in the car and headed toward my place. He didn't turn on any music, so it made the situation awkward. I felt uncomfortable, but refused to be the first person to speak.

"Since I'm the man, I guess I should be the one to break the ice," Casper said.

I pretended to be engrossed with whatever was outside the window. He continued to say, "You don't have to talk. Just listen."

I turned my attention to him. "Let's get something straight. You don't control me. I can talk when I want to and listen when I want to."

"Gotcha." He laughed.

I had been hoodwinked.

"I was wondering if I could get you to talk. I'm sorry."

I folded my arms. "You should be," I growled.

"Don't get me wrong. I'm not sorry for telling you how I feel. I'm just sorry you're denying yourself."

I interrupted. "You're so full of yourself. You might be used to women throwing themselves at you, but this woman does not and will not be part of your harem."

"I'm not dating anyone else," he said without hesitating.

"According to *People* magazine, MTV, and BET, you are always dating someone."

The tone in Casper's voice changed. He said, "If you want to know anything about me, ask me. I know you're not used to it, but no matter what, I will always tell you the truth."

"Yeah right," I snapped.

"Believe what you want," he responded.

"I call it as I see it."

"If that's the case, you will admit that you're drawn to me."

I responded, "I need you like I need a hole in my head."

"Feisty aren't we?" Casper joked.

"Can you turn on some music please? I need to clear my head," I asked, and turned my head to look out the window.

"Your wish is my command."

The sounds of the R & B singer Ne-Yo blasted through the speakers. Casper played several other songs that I liked. If he was trying to break down my resistance, I wasn't having it. I was not going to let him get next to me. The closer we got to my house, the more I realized that there was more to Casper than a handsome face. There was something special about him. But I didn't want to admit it to him or myself.

When we pulled up in my driveway, he beat me to

opening my car door. He held his hand out and said, "Let me."

I placed my hand in his as I got out of the car. He closed the door behind me and began walking with me to the front door. "I got it from here," I stated.

"I want to make sure you get in safely."

I didn't respond. I allowed him to hold my hand as we walked to the door. I fumbled for my keys and dropped them before unlocking the door. We both reached down to pick them up and bumped heads. "Ouch," we said in unison.

I rubbed the top of my head. "Are you okay?" Casper asked.

"I'm fine. A little bump is nothing," I reassured him. "Wait here while I turn the alarm off," I stated after unlocking the door.

When I returned, he was standing outside of the doorway.

"All's secure." I saluted him.

"Good. I didn't want to pull out my karate moves." Casper made a crazy move resembling something off a movie.

I laughed and said, "I'm sure that would have been a sight."

"Come lock the door," he commanded.

When I reached the door, before I could react, Casper leaned down and planted a sensuous kiss on my lips. The fire that ignited within my soul left me speechless. "Your kisses are just like I imagined, sweet as brown sugar," Casper stated before turning to walk away.

He left me standing there in a trance. My fingers brushed my lips as I savored his luscious lips on top of mine. The kiss lingered on my lips. I locked the door and turned on the alarm. I skipped up the stairs to my bedroom. My cell phone rang and I became disappointed when I heard Carmen's voice on the other end, instead of Casper's. "How did it go?" Carmen asked.

"Darn it Carmen, you must have the paparazzi giving you my every move. I just walked in the door."

She laughed. "It must have gone better than I hoped."

"Oh no you don't. It was a business dinner. Nothing more." I wouldn't dare admit anything else to Carmen.

"My, my. Somebody is sure on the defensive."

"I can't help it if you're as nosy as they come."

"It's my job to know what's going on."

"Well, you're fired," I said.

Carmen yawned. "I'll pretend I didn't hear that."

I prepared to tell Carmen about my date. If I didn't, I knew she wouldn't let me sleep. I recounted our dinner conversation, leaving out the kiss.

"You go girl," Carmen said, sounding more excited about my date than I did.

"See, that's why I didn't want to tell you. Now you're getting these funny ideas in your head."

"Live a little. Casper is just what you need to get out of the rut you're in."

"I'm happy with my life just the way it is."

Carmen said, "Come on. You can't tell me you didn't enjoy the attention."

I curled up under the covers and said, "Well . . . kind of."

"I knew it," Carmen exclaimed.

"Don't go reading more into it than what's there," I reminded her.

"It's clear to me that you two will be making more than beautiful music together."

"Now don't even go there."

"I did. And you and Casper will too. On that note, good night," Carmen said, before disconnecting the call.

She loves to get the last word in. I clicked the phone and was about to call Carmen back, but decided not to. I was disappointed that Casper didn't call. I thought about him so much that he invaded my dreams. I kept dreaming about the restaurant, the talk, and the kiss. In my dream, the kiss lasted longer and led to us wrapped in each other's arms. When I woke up, I was kissing the pillow. I threw it on the floor and yelled, "I need to get a grip."

After my morning ritual of exercising, I took a long hot shower. I retrieved the daily paper from the bushes, placed it under my arm and strolled to the kitchen. I poured a bowl of raisin bran and before sitting at the counter, I turned on the TV. I caught the tail end of Star's show. I liked her show because it was informative and she was not afraid to stand up for what was right.

In between watching TV and eating my cereal, I read the paper. When I got to the entertainment section, I spit out my cereal. A picture of me and Casper walking out of L'Orangerie stared back at me.

"What in the world." I muted out the sounds of the TV and read the headline. MIMI DID IT, PARRIS'S DOING IT: OLDER WOMEN, YOUNGER MEN—IS THIS THE LATEST FAD?

I read the article and was appalled that people assumed we were dating. My main question was how did they even know we were there. The phone rang. I dropped the paper on the counter and answered.

"Parris did you see today's paper yet?" Carmen asked.

"Yes and I'm livid. Something told me going out with him wasn't a good idea," I said with flared nostrils.

"Calm down."

"Carmen, you know how I value my privacy."

"Girl, please, this is the best thing that could have happened."

"I disagree."

"I'm about to milk this publicity for what it's worth," Carmen said. It sounded like she was typing.

"I bet you Sandy is behind this. I thought I saw a car following us last night."

"Why didn't you say anything?" Carmen asked.

"Like it would have mattered," I snapped. My other line rang. "Hold on Carmen." I clicked over.

"Parris, I'm so sorry." It was Casper.

I said, "Hold on." I clicked back over to Carmen. "That's Casper, I really need to find out if he had anything to do with this."

"I'm sure he didn't. Don't worry; I'll get a press release out that will put a smile back on your face."

I clicked back over and without giving Casper a chance, I lashed out at him. "Did you have anything to do with the article in today's paper!?"

"I called to check on you, not to get fussed at," he responded.

"I'm sorry."

"After our conversation last night, you should at least know I wouldn't do something that crazy. I don't like people all in my personal affairs."

"Neither do I," I responded.

We both held the phone. In what seemed to be our normal routine, he broke the silence. "Parris, after talking to you last night, I knew seeing this in the paper would bother you."

"You think you know me so well after only talking to me a few times?" I challenged.

"One day you'll realize we have more things in common than music."

His statement reminded me of the kiss. I momentarily forgot about the article and changed the subject. "Speaking of music, when do you want to go into the studio?" I asked.

Casper paused and responded, "Today if you're up to it."

"Give me directions. I'll meet you there around two," I said.

"I can come pick you up."

"That won't be necessary," I responded. I found something to write with as he recited the directions.

He added, "You have my cell number, so if you get lost call me."

"If you gave good directions, I shouldn't get lost."

"Then I'll see you at two."

"Bye," I said with a grin across my face. I forgot all about the article. My mind filled with thoughts of Casper and our kiss.

The trance soon broke when the house phone rang. I glanced at the caller ID and UNKNOWN displayed on the phone. I hesitated but answered. Sandy's irritating voice sounded from the other end. "Parris, can I *now* get that interview?"

I didn't entertain her with an answer. I slammed the phone down.

9

NICE AND SLOW

Casper gave good directions, but it took me thirty extra minutes to get to his studio because I had to dodge the paparazzi. When I reached the parking garage, a buff security guard asked for my ID. He scanned his printout and confirmed my name on the visitor's list. I was impressed with their security.

Before exiting the car, I applied another coat of chocolate Mac lip gloss. I ran my hands through my hair to loosen up some of the curls. With one shake of my head, the curls fell perfectly in place. I pressed the number ten on the elevator. The sight of Casper took my breath away. Although he was casually dressed, he looked tantalizing in his Sean John sportswear. "Glad you made it safely." He leaned down and hugged me after I exited the elevator.

Someone behind him cleared his throat. "Aren't you going to introduce us?" a heavyset man asked, as he extended his hand.

I shook his hand.

"I'm Peter Grayson."

"Nice to meet you," I responded.

"The pleasure is all mine."

"Yeah, yeah." Casper interrupted, draping his arm around my shoulders, as we followed Peter to the back.

Casper was a little too close for comfort. I didn't want to make a scene, so I didn't remove his arm. My senses were heightened as the smell of his Unforgivable cologne traveled up my nostrils.

"You can put your things over there." Casper pointed to a small table in the corner and a coatrack.

I removed my short blue jacket and placed the jacket and purse on the coatrack. Peter went behind the walls and started messing with the controls. I followed Casper into a booth.

"This is a nice studio. So is this where all the hits happen?" I asked.

"Some. I travel and I do a lot of it at home."

"I see," I said, as I watched him prepare for our session.

Casper stopped and said, "I would have invited you over to my place, but the paparazzi's camped outside of it."

I frowned. "I've had enough of them to last me a lifetime."

"Enough about them. I'm hoping you're ready to complete that song you were singing last night in the car," Casper said. His eyes sparkled.

"The question is, are you ready?" I flirted. I forgot about the paparazzi and concentrated on him. He handed me a pair of headphones.

"If you're up for the challenge, I am," he responded.

With confidence, I blurted, "Let's do this."

"Go into the booth. Wait for my signal and then show me what you got," Casper said, with authority.

Little did he know I wanted to show him more than my musical talents. Just in case he was watching, I added a few more twists to my walk. When I turned to close the door, I caught him drooling. Busted. I couldn't help myself. I winked before closing the door. I pulled out a few sheets of paper with the song lyrics from my pocket as backup. It had been a while since I was in the studio and, adding Casper's presence, the pressure was on.

"Go ahead, songbird," I heard Casper say through the headphones.

I cleared my throat, closed my eyes, and began to sing,

> *My heart is singing a sad sad song . . .*
> *My heart is wondering what is going on . . .*
> *Every time I think that I found the one for me . . .*
> *Something reveals itself and leaves me feeling oh*
>   *so lonely.*
>
> *My mind is telling me to leave you alone . . .*
> *My mind's so confused, Can't tell right from*
>   *wrong . . .*
> *But every time I think about leaving you alone . . .*
> *Something pulls me back into your arms . . .*

After I sang the song, Casper played it back to me with his music. "Ms. Lady, how does it sound?"

His face wrinkled anticipating my response. I let him sweat for a minute. I crossed my arms. A smile swept across my face. "I love it. I see why you're *the man*."

He swung his chair around. Peter gave us both the thumbs up signal. We worked on perfecting the song for the remainder of the evening. After I laid my vocals, I went behind the booth and watched Casper work his magic. He's a genius and to think I almost let my pride get in the way.

"I'm about to order Chinese. Y'all want something?" Peter asked.

Before I could answer, Casper responded, "Naw, man. We're about through here. Parris and I have other plans."

"You don't have to treat me to dinner. I'll swing by and pick up something on my way home," I said.

"I know I don't have to. I want to," he said, as he swung his chair around and faced me.

I felt trapped. "Casper, you seem to be a nice guy. But I don't know if I'm ready for anything more than friendship right now."

His eyes sparkled when he said, "All I want is for you to be happy."

"I'm happy. I just don't see our relationship developing beyond a professional one." He took my hand and kissed each finger. My reserves were melting, but I stood firm. "Casper, Peter will be back any minute."

"He knows how I feel about you." He placed my hand over his heart before continuing. "Because you have my heart, I don't mind taking it nice and slow with you. I have plenty of patience."

I jerked my hand away feeling dazed and confused. "My patience is thin these days."

"Then it means you'll stop running from how you really feel soon," Casper said with confidence.

Peter walked back in before I could respond. I felt embarrassed. I took the bottled water Peter offered me and gulped it down. I walked out of the room. I didn't hear what transpired between Peter and Casper, but before I could get my jacket on, Casper was waiting for me by the exit door.

"Ready?" he asked.

Tired and not wanting to cause a scene in front of Peter, I responded, "Sure. I'll follow you."

When we got into our respective cars, Casper called me on my cell. "Change of plans, why don't you follow me to my place and I'll cook you a home-cooked meal."

I hesitated, but thought it would be a perfect time to see him in his own environment. "Sure, but what about the media?"

"I forgot about them." He paused. "There's a back way. Follow me. If for some reason we get separated, drive down Roundtree Boulevard and then call me on my cell."

"Lead the way," I said, before disconnecting the call.

Normally, when I drive, I listen to music to clear my head. Because I didn't want to get lost, I concentrated on keeping up with Casper. I could tell he was driving extra slow for me. I was tempted to call him and tell him to speed up, but didn't. "What am I getting myself into?" I blurted out.

The phone rang and BARBARA ANN, my mom's name, displayed across the screen. I debated on whether to answer or let it go to voice mail, and finally picked up.

"She's alive," Barbara Ann sarcastically said.

Casper increased his pace as I attempted to juggle following him and talking on the phone. "I'm sorry for not calling," I said.

"No big deal. You just forgot about the woman who

fed and birthed you." Although I had heard the story many times before, I didn't interrupt her. I listened to her complain as I maneuvered through traffic.

"Mom, I've been working on my new CD."

"That's still no excuse not to call."

"I know and I'm apologizing," I said, although I wanted to say, "What more do you want from me?" but didn't, because I would have regretted it the moment the words were out of my mouth.

"Call me when you *find the time.*"

I was in a dead zone, so the call dropped. I stared at the phone when my mom didn't respond. I almost missed seeing Casper exit the freeway. I hit the speed dial. "Mama, I'm sorry. I've been under so much pressure."

Sniffling, she responded, "You know I worry about you."

"I know. I've been wrapped up in my own little world and should have called. At the very least to check up on you," I said, honestly feeling guilty.

"Sweetie, no need to apologize. I'm a little emotional right now."

I followed Casper through a side street, before turning into a garage. "What's wrong?"

"It's this medicine the doctor has me on. My hormones and emotions are all out of whack."

I parked behind Casper. He got out and walked to the car door.

"Do you need me to come down there?" I asked.

"No. My body just needs time to adjust to my new medication."

Casper tapped on the window. I rolled the window down and covered the receiver. "It's my mom. I'll be out in a minute."

"Take your time. You can pull up on the side of me," he said, before returning to his car and opening one of the garage doors.

"Why don't you come to LA? A change of scenery might do you good." I drove my car beside Casper's into his spacious garage. There was a window showing another connecting garage which showcased two other vehicles—the Jaguar and a raven-black Corvette.

"Parris are you listening to me?" Barbara Ann asked.

"Yes. I'm sorry. I'm over at this producer's place . . . well never mind." I cut myself off.

"You know how I hate planes."

"I know, but it's too far for you to be driving."

"I'll think about it."

"Please do."

Casper patiently waited for me. I used my hand to motion to him that I would only be another minute. "Mom, I hate to go, but I have to."

I ended the call before she could go into a lecture about Archie. She never let me forget the huge mistake I made with him. Casper opened my door and held his hand out for me to hold. I got out and followed him into his house.

As we walked through the huge kitchen, I noticed for a bachelor, his place was well decorated. The living room looked as if it could have come from the pages of *Better Homes and Gardens* with his tan leather sofa and matching chairs. He appeared to be into Safari prints, because there was a Safari rug and throw. The carpet was a golden brown and although I had my shoes on, it felt plush as we walked through it. "Wow. Your place is immaculate."

He stuck his chest out with pride. "I'll give you the grand tour in a minute. I need to check the front."

When he left me, I walked around picking up African figurines. "These are nice," I said, as I continued to look around the room.

I opened up the huge wooden connecting doors and ventured into another room. A huge cherrywood desk and an extensive library of books and CDs indicated it was his office. I scanned the bookshelf. Books by Marcus Garvey, Langston Hughes, Richard Wright, and many more adorned the shelves. Some of the authors I had heard of and plenty I hadn't.

Impressed by the music awards scattered throughout the room, I hoped he could do for me what he'd done for so many other artists. His scent alerted me that he was behind me. "I couldn't resist exploring," I said, while turning around.

"I can give you the full tour now if you like." He extended his arm.

I looped my arm through his as we walked. "Were the paparazzi camped out?"

"No. Looks like they got tired and left."

We both laughed. I followed him down some stairs. He flipped the light switch. I was amazed to see a room that would put any studio to shame. "This is my favorite spot in the house," he said.

"This is nice," I said, admiring his home studio.

He pressed a button and music came blasting out of the speakers. I played a few bars of another song in my head on the keyboards. When Casper wrapped his arms around me, I felt there was no other place I would rather be. He continued to hold me as I played the song on the keyboards. We were caught up in the moment.

His cell phone vibrated breaking the trance. To my dismay, he released me and answered his phone.

Saved by the bell. I couldn't explain what was happening to me. It was probably one of his many women he denied having who was calling him. I needed to get a grip. He wasn't my man. It shouldn't matter who was on the phone. I pretended to be looking through a magazine while attempting to decipher his end of the conversation.

"Jean, it's over. Stop calling me," he said, barely above a whisper. He rubbed his bald head. I'm sure he didn't mean for it to be erotic, but the thought of me rubbing his head flashed through my mind and caused me to squirm.

"Lose my number. I know you can't call my house, because I blocked you." Casper's voice escalated. "I have company and this conversation is over." He clicked his phone off.

"Somebody sure has you riled up." I couldn't help but tease, hoping he would elaborate so I would know what I was getting myself into.

"That was an ex. Nothing to worry about." He walked toward me, but I held my hand out and halted him from getting closer.

Oh no, he wasn't getting off that easy. "From your end of the conversation, it didn't sound like it was over to me," I stated. Ooops. I didn't mean to let him know I had been listening.

He smiled. "So you do care?"

"Hey, this is not about me mister." I crossed my arms.

He sat down in a black swivel chair with a grin plastered on his face. His expression soon changed as he spoke, "Jean was somebody I used to date. I overheard her tell one of her girlfriends about her plans on getting pregnant."

"Sounds like she had it all planned out." I found myself gravitating toward him. I was standing in front of him. He opened his legs and pulled me onto his lap.

"Some of my boys had told me to watch out for her, but when she was around me, she never showed signs of being a gold digger."

"They never do," I said. Looking into his eyes was like getting a peek into his soul. Clearly enthralled not just in the story, but, in hearing his sexy voice, I asked, "So what did you do next?"

"I dragged it out for a few weeks. I started asking her to do stuff. Just to see how far she would go to please me."

"What happened next?" I asked. Casper's fingers gently caressed my hair. I was losing my ground with him.

"She got tired of being my slave and started telling me no."

I couldn't keep myself from laughing. "No, she didn't."

Casper flashed a smile I felt was reserved just for me. "I told her I couldn't be with a woman who didn't take care of my every wish."

I removed his hand from my hair. I rolled my eyes and said, "Oh really now."

"I had to. But the story doesn't end there. After I broke up with her, she begged me to take her back. She said she would do anything and she meant *anything*," Casper said, as he planted kisses on my neck.

"She has some serious issues," I said, with my head bent back enjoying the feel of his lips on my neck.

"Yes, and when she said that, I had to lay it out on the line and let her know I knew how scandalous she really was."

"And now she's blowing your phone off the hook."

"It's been about six months since I last heard from her."

"I guess the picture in the paper sparked her interest," I blurted.

"Who cares? Enough about Jean, it's all about you," he stated before reaching up and bringing my lips to his. He slid his tongue into my mouth and we were like one. I don't know how long we kissed. There was no mistake about it, I was losing ground.

Casper was the first to pull away. He took his finger and ran it across my lips. "Parris if we don't stop, I won't be able to."

"It's only a kiss." I flirted.

"Your kisses are lethal." He laughed. My heart skipped a beat.

I removed his arms and stood up. "Where's the dinner you promised me?" It was getting hot and that's the only thing I could think of to say. I went toward the stairway.

"I'll whip us up something real quick." I heard him say as he followed me up the stairs.

"I need to use your restroom." I needed to get away quick. I was losing all my reserves when it came to Casper. When I got in the bathroom, I closed the door and locked it. I attempted to close the toilet seat without making a sound before sitting on top of it.

"What have I gotten myself into?" I asked myself. I looked at my gold Movado watch. He probably thought I was stinking up his bathroom as long as I had been in here. I pulled myself together. I flushed the toilet and to camouflage I sprayed the room with the air freshener. I turned the water on and washed my hands.

Casper was in the kitchen with an apron on. The

sight of him cooking was a turn on. "Do you need any help?" I offered.

"No, dear. I have it all under control."

The way he said dear, made my toes curl. "You sure? I can cut up some of those vegetables for you."

"All I want you to do is sit and look pretty," he responded.

With confidence, I said, "That's not hard to do."

"I like this side of you," he said.

"I'm just being me."

"And you being you turns me on," he said as our eyes locked. The timer on the stove broke the trance.

10

A LITTLE SOMETHING-SOMETHING

"This is delicious," I said in between mouth-watering bites of steak. "You're a good cook."

"I can do a little something-something," Casper said, as he stuck out his chest.

"A way into a woman's heart is through her stomach." I challenged him.

"In that case, let me cook for you *every* day." His eyes sparkled.

We ate in silence. I ravished the baked potato piled with sour cream, shredded cheese, and bacon bits. I normally don't eat bread, but couldn't resist his homemade rolls. "I can't eat another bite." I wiped my mouth with the silver napkin that matched the silver tablecloth.

Casper asked, "What about dessert?"

"I'll have to take a rain check. I'm so full. If I eat anything else, I'll burst." I rubbed my stomach.

"I'll hold you to it."

"Deal." I stood up to take my dishes to the kitchen.

"Leave them. I got it."

"In my house, whoever didn't cook, washes the dishes," I stated.

He hesitated at first, but said, "Only if you insist."

"After such a wonderful dinner, that's the least I could do."

"I can think of other ways to be thanked," he responded.

Casper helped me take the dishes to the kitchen. While I washed, he dried. The conversation remained light. I glanced at the big black round clock in the kitchen. "It's getting late. I better be going," I said.

He wiped his hands on the dish towel and said, "Thank you."

"No need to thank me," I responded, although I was confused as to why he was thanking me.

He placed my hand in his, lifted it up to his mouth and kissed the back of it. "You've made tonight special for me."

"You're a special guy." I forced myself to smile although I felt like running away.

"I promise if you give me the opportunity to show you how special you are, you won't regret it."

I stuttered. "I need to find my purse. I really must go now."

He released my hand and shook his head. "The lady keeps running away."

I don't know how I avoided the paparazzi and made it home, because after leaving Casper's I was in a daze. Things were happening in a whirlwind spin. One minute we meet, the next minute Casper's producing for me, and the next we're kissing and he's cooking me dinner.

Maybe the doctor should increase the dosage of my antidepressants. Who am I fooling? There's no medicine that can solve this problem. A part of me wanted to open up to Casper and let the chips fall wherever, but the other part of me remembered how much love could hurt.

To my dismay, Casper didn't make any more advances toward me over the next few weeks. It would have been easier if we weren't working together in the studio during this time. After each session, I would watch Casper work his magic and we would listen to the finished product and either agree or disagree before moving on to another song.

"I need to redo those vocals," I said, after hearing how the last track came out.

"It sounds fine to me," Peter commented.

"She's right. I think she can do better than that," Casper interjected.

I went back into the booth. "I'm ready. Let's take it from the top."

"Remember, this is a blues tune. Let me feel it," Casper spoke into my head piece.

I walked up to the microphone and sang.

I got a feeling . . .
That something, something just ain't right . . .
I got a funny funny feeling . . .
That you're creeping through the night . . .

When I was satisfied that the vocals were right, I stopped singing and the look across Casper's face said it all. Casper said, "I got a feeling this is another hit."

"You sure know how to pump up my ego."

"I'm only speaking the truth."

We spent the next few hours making sure the track met both of our approvals.

Casper left the room to use the restroom. As I gathered up my things, a woman dressed in a tight low-cut blouse and black leather miniskirt walked in. To me she looked like a video vixen. I chastised myself for thinking that of my fellow sister.

"I know he's in there. So why don't you stop lying?" she slurred.

I turned to leave, but stopped when she directed her words toward me. "So you're the old woman my man's been creeping with."

I'm a low-key, nonviolent woman, so I ignored her and walked toward the elevator.

"Oh, I know you heard me. I don't see what he wants with your old behind anyway," she blurted.

I'm thinking to myself *Where is Casper?* Apparently, the woman needed me to check her. I turned around and said, "Look, Miss. This old woman doesn't have time to play childish games."

It looked as if she was about to run up on me, but Casper came from around the corner and grabbed her by her arms, before she could move farther. "Jean, you need to get a grip," he said.

"So is that the thing you left me for?" Jean screamed.

Casper responded, "I left you because of you."

She jerked her hand away. "I can't believe this."

Casper had a vicious look on his face and it scared me. "Don't ever show up here or at my place again. If

I hear about you threatening my woman, I will take care of you myself."

"Go to hell Casper." She halted, looked me up and down, and said, "And, don't think you can hold on to him. If I couldn't, as old as you are, you definitely can't."

She stormed off, brushing past me. I was about to go after her and pull on her fake horse hair, but Casper intervened. "She's not worth it," he reassured me.

"You're right. But she better hope I don't see her outside, because I don't mind giving her an old-school butt whooping," I said, angrier than I had been in a long time.

Peter's laughter stopped me from completing my statement. He asked, "Is she what you ladies call ghetto-fabulous?"

Casper and I exchanged looks. I laughed and responded, "Yes."

After the Jean incident at the studio, Casper went out of his way to assure me she was only a lunatic ex-girl-friend and not a current love interest. I pretended to not care one way or another, but I did. I allowed him to dote on me. We agreed that going forward, we would juggle time between the office and his home studio.

A few hours before I was scheduled to meet Casper at his home studio, a florist delivered several tropical floral arrangements. I tipped the deliveryman and opened the card. *Sorry about the incident last night at the studio. Here's a little something to make up for it. Parris, give US a chance.*

You have my heart.

I held the card to my chest and closed my eyes. "Lord, I know I prayed for you to send me a man who would love and protect me. What am I to do? I don't know if I can trust myself around him. I need you to direct my steps." Barely above a whisper, I continued, "And protect my heart."

The first few nights working from Casper's studio went fine. We avoided being alone for any lengthy period of time. Several times we caught ourselves in compromising positions, but Peter being there helped us keep our professional stance. Casper announced his plans for the weekend and they didn't include me. With him being occupied entertaining his brother, I would have a break from singing and time away from Casper. My heart sank. Casper walked me to my car. Before opening my car door, he asked, "Would you mind attending the party with me and Xavier on Saturday night?"

I hesitated before answering, "What time will you be picking me up?"

He released his breath. "I'll pick you up for dinner around eight and we can go to it from there."

"I look forward to it."

"Me too." He leaned down and I thought he was going to kiss me, so I puckered up my lips. Instead he leaned down and whispered in my ear. "By the way, I see you've stopped running."

I blushed. I opened the car door and got in.

"See you on Saturday," he said.

I waved before driving off.

11

UPSIDE DOWN

"Carmen, please. You have to go with me," I said.

"When you admit you have feelings for Casper, I'll go. Otherwise girlie, you're on your own." Carmen turned away.

We were at a day spa in Beverly Hills. I tossed and turned the previous night and needed a small retreat. Carmen didn't hesitate to join me after I mentioned it was my treat. Although Casper and I were not in a relationship, meeting someone's family was serious. I needed Carmen as a buffer. She continued to enjoy her manicure as my feet felt as if I could float on them after receiving a pedicure.

"Please, do me this one little favor," I begged.

Carmen blinked her eyes showing off her newly applied fake eyelashes. "I stand by my word."

I was getting antsy, so I had to do something. "Fine."

"Did I hear something?" she toyed.

"I have feelings for Casper," I blurted. "There I said it."

The manicurist messed up one of Carmen's nails when she waved it in the air. "I knew it."

Relief swept through my body for the simple fact I allowed myself to admit it. "Shh. You don't have to tell the world," I chastised her.

"Girl, we need to hurry up and get out of here. I need a new outfit. I need a pair of shoes."

"Don't use my situation as an excuse to shop."

"I will and have. When we leave here, we're headed to Rodeo."

"I'll pass."

Carmen said, "Not this time."

"Did someone ever tell you, you're good at manipulating people?"

"All the time." Carmen laughed.

I followed suit.

I hadn't talked to Casper since Friday morning. I dialed his number. "Did I catch you at a bad time?"

"Not at all," he responded in a husky voice.

"I invited Carmen to come with us tonight. I hope you don't mind."

He paused. "Of course not. I'll let my brother know."

"I forgot to ask you. Is your brother married?"

"Hold on, I'll let you ask him yourself."

Before I could protest, Xavier's voice was speaking from the other end of the phone. "I've heard a lot about you."

"Don't believe everything you hear." I joked.

"It was all good. So you had a question for me?"

One thing about those Johnson men, they don't beat around the bush. I cleared my throat. "I wanted to know if you were married."

"Hmm. It depends on what day it is."

I couldn't tell if he was joking or not. I could hear Casper in the background telling him to answer the question. "No. I'm divorced. I don't have any kids and I'm looking. Can you hook a brotha up?"

"I'm not a matchmaker, but there are plenty of available women in this town. I'm sure if you look half as good as your brother, you won't have a problem finding one."

"Call up one of your friends for me."

"Give me one good reason to do that." I teased.

"I have several but I don't think my brother will appreciate me telling his girl about my positive attributes."

Xavier was cool. He didn't act like I was a celebrity. I told him about Carmen. He assured me he could handle her. We joked for a few more minutes before he handed the phone back to Casper.

"I like him," I said.

Casper sounded surprised, "You do? That's good to know."

I needed extra time to get ready so I rushed off the phone. "I'm not going to hold you. I'll see you tonight."

"Bye, sexy."

Why was I blushing like a teenager?

Carmen agreed to meet me at my house. It would make it easier on everyone around. After exiting the shower, I layered my body with Issey Miyake lotion and sprayed the perfume over my pulse areas. I bought a new outfit earlier, but decided to save it for another time. I went through my closet and decided on a sexy crimson-red Dolce & Gabbana halter dress that stopped right above the knee. A pair of ankle-strapped pumps completed my sexy assemble.

At 7:45, Carmen arrived. She sashayed in looking good in her short black Versace pleated dress. She held a black Prada leather handbag under her arms. "Sorry, I'm late. There was an accident on the 405 and then I almost ran out of gas."

"Slow down," I said as I hugged her.

"Casper better watch out. You're a knockout in that dress," Carmen stated.

"You're looking good yourself. I love those shoes," I said, admiring the studded T-strap sandals she was wearing.

"I told you to get a pair."

"Now you know I have to be unique. If you have it, I don't want it." I laughed.

"I need to freshen up before they get here," Carmen said.

"You know where everything is," I responded. I went back upstairs to exchange purses. There wasn't a clasp on the red nylon handbag, but it matched my outfit. I placed my ID, cell phone, and makeup bag into it.

I heard a faint knock on the door. "Come in," I yelled.

Carmen walked in and plopped down in the chaise in the corner. "I love this chair. Are you excited about your date?"

"Yes and no. Believe it or not, this is only our third official date."

"But you guys have been spending a lot of time together." She crossed her ankles and held out her hands admiring her freshly manicured nails. "I should have gotten another color."

"Fuchsia is a pretty color." I ignored her first comment.

"Yeah, but it doesn't go with everything. I'll probably have it redone on Monday."

"Would you like a drink while we wait on the guys?"

"Sure. Bring me back up a wine spritzer."

I picked up a small pillow off my bed and threw it at her. She ducked. I said, "You better get your behind up and come downstairs."

While we were going down the stairs, the doorbell rang. I panicked. "How do I look?" I turned around facing Carmen.

"You look great," she reassured me.

"What about my breath?" I put my hands over my mouth and blew.

"Smells just like a baby's bottom." Carmen teased.

"Oh no. I have to go back upstairs."

Before I could finish, Carmen grabbed my arm. "Girl, you look good, you smell good, and your breath is not foul, so answer the door."

I ran my hand over the bottom of my dress. When I opened the door, Carmen and I both were in for a treat. Standing outside had to be the two handsomest men in the state of California. I looked at Carmen and I could see the twinkle in her eyes.

Casper joked. "Are you going to let us in? Or should we go and come back?"

I hugged him. Casper walked in followed by Xavier.

"So you're the lady who has my brother singing love songs?"

I extended my hand out to Xavier and he pulled me in for a hug.

Casper cleared his throat and said, "If you weren't my brother, I would have to hurt you."

"Beautiful women have always been my downfall," Xavier was quick to say. "And who do we have here?"

He took Carmen's extended hand and kissed the back of it.

"Xavier, this is my best friend Carmen Grisby."

"Nice to meet you," Carmen graciously said.

Xavier, still holding Carmen's hand, said, "The pleasure is all mine."

Casper and I exchanged looks. He spoke, "Ladies, our chariot awaits."

Xavier and Carmen walked out. I set the alarm and was startled when Casper whisked me into his arms. He said, "I hope you didn't think a hug was enough."

He touched my chin and brought my mouth up to his. "That's much better."

"Casss-per," I moaned.

"Yes, dear," he said, without releasing me.

"Your brother and my friend are waiting for us."

The warning beep from the alarm went off. He released me. "Come on let's go before we're surrounded by law enforcement."

A long black gold-trimmed limousine awaited us. Carmen leaned and whispered in my ear. "I'm glad I talked you into inviting me."

Once settled, we were each handed a red rose. Xavier poured some champagne into four glasses. We held our glasses together for a toast.

"To the luckiest men in the world," Xavier toasted.

Casper faced me and said, "To the woman who holds my heart."

I don't know if it was the champagne or the company, but ever since the day Casper Johnson entered my life, he's turned my world upside down.

12

BABY BOY

At dinner I got a chance to see how Casper interacted with his brother. Casper was the youngest in his family. To his embarrassment, Xavier recanted a few of his childhood stories that kept us all in stitches. Before we left the restaurant to go to the party, Carmen and I made a detour to the ladies' room. I reapplied my lipstick.

Carmen brushed her hair and said, "Girl, baby boy is head over heels in love with you and you're too blind to see it."

I puckered my lips to make sure I didn't miss a spot. "He's infatuated."

"You might not know the difference but I do."

"I'm not ready for a committed relationship."

"That's what your mouth says."

I looked at Carmen, rolled my eyes and left her in the bathroom brushing her hair. "Carmen will be out in a minute," I said as I looped my arm through Casper's.

I was unaware that she was right behind me. She said, "I'm ready."

We enjoyed a peaceful ride to one of Casper's colleague's birthday party. When we arrived, there were more luxury cars than in a European car lot. Carmen and I exchanged looks. It looked more like a playboy fest. Most of the women's dresses were low-cut and short, leaving barely enough room for the imagination. If they had on pants, they were as tight as a second skin. Casper stayed by my side. I didn't want to appear as if I was crowding him, so I said, "Go ahead and mingle. Carmen and I will be over there."

When I turned around, Carmen was nowhere to be found. Neither was Xavier.

"There are a few people I want to introduce you to first," Casper stated. He held my hand as he led me to the other side of the room.

"Stanley, this is Parris."

He moved the all-too-willing young female from his lap and stood up to shake my hand. "Parris, I've been meaning to talk to you about coming over to my label. I understand your contract is nearly up."

Word traveled fast. I responded, "Yes. It is. I may or may not re-sign."

Stanley walked closer and put his arm around my shoulders. "Now you have choices." He reached into his pocket and handed me a card. "Have your agent call me next week."

He directed his next statement at Casper, "Thank you, man, for making the introduction. I'll forever be grateful."

Casper responded, "No problem."

When we walked away, I asked, "What was that

all about? I wasn't even aware he was interested in signing me."

"He was in the studio one day when Peter was mixing and heard one of your new songs," Casper responded.

I dropped the card inside my purse. "I'll give this to Carmen later."

Casper introduced me to a few more people. From what I knew of him thus far, I assessed he was well respected. I stood in a corner and watched Casper mingle. He didn't want to leave me, but I insisted he network. Besides, I wanted to see how he would react when I wasn't by his side.

I wasn't hungry, but found myself sampling the appetizers. Caviar was being served and to this day, I couldn't see how people eat the stuff. I tried it once but after I threw up on everybody around me, I vowed not to try it again. Casper seemed to be handling himself well as women threw themselves at him. I could tell he was uncomfortable, but I refused to come to his rescue. He caught me watching him and motioned for me to help. When he batted those eyes at me, I was helpless. I made my way through the crowd of people. He leaned down and planted a kiss on my lips. The smile I gave spoke volumes. Without mouthing a word, it said, "Ladies, he's mine."

The women he dismissed were pissed. I heard one say, "Who does she think she is?"

Casper grabbed my hand. I turned around and winked at him. As we walked away, I heard one of them say, "That's Parris the singer."

"I don't care who she is. I had my eyes on him first," the other one said.

"My, my. These ladies are vicious," I stated and giggled.

We stopped so Casper could speak to someone. He introduced me, but my attention was elsewhere. I scanned the room to see if I could locate Carmen or Xavier. No luck. Who I did see, almost made me lose my balance.

I tugged on Casper's sleeve. He bent down. "I'll be back. I see someone I need to talk to," I said, without waiting for him to respond.

Dexter, my ex-manager, was busy talking to a group of people and didn't see me walk up.

I spoke. Dexter turned around and almost spilled his drink. "Parris?" He hugged me so tight I felt like I was going to burst.

I responded, "Dex. It's so good to see you."

"It's been a long time." He turned back to the group of people and said, "Excuse me. I need to talk to this lady."

As we walked to find a less congested area, we talked. "You're looking good, Dex."

"Hold up," he said as he got a server's attention. He took two glasses of champagne. "This is cause for a celebration."

We clinked our glasses. I saw Casper out the corner of my eye. He didn't approach, but his gaze never left my location. I had to put Casper out of my mind for a moment and take care of the business at hand.

"Dex. I've been praying for this opportunity," I said.

He tried to stop me. "You don't have to."

I interrupted him. "I let a man take over my life and in turn, made some bad decisions."

He drank his champagne. "You weren't the first and won't be the last. Trust me. I don't hold it against you."

"You don't have to hold back on my account. I shouldn't have dropped you."

"Listen, baby girl, when I discovered you, I knew you were going to be a star and I would be the one to take you there. Once I did that, my job was done. The only regret I have is that Archie hurt you and I couldn't stop him."

Tears started flowing down my cheeks. "Dexter, you don't know how it's eaten me up that I . . ."

"Not another word about it. The past is in the past." He interrupted and hugged me.

By this time, Casper was near us. He asked, "Parris, are you all right?"

Dexter released me. I wiped the tears from my face. I responded, "I'm fine now."

Dexter extended his hand as I made the introduction, "This is my ex-manager, Dexter Ringo. The man who made me a star."

"Casper Johnson."

"CJ, the Hitmaker. I've heard all about you."

They forgot I was standing there. They started talking about people they knew. I watched. I was ecstatic to see Dexter. For the second time in my life, I owed him my gratitude. Years ago, he took a chance on me, but tonight he cleared my conscience.

"Fellows, I need to go to the ladies' room," I said, not wanting to interrupt their male bonding.

Dexter pulled out his card and handed it to me. "Don't be a stranger."

I kissed him on the cheek and said, "I won't."

After I found an available bathroom, I went out on the balcony in read of returning to the party.

"Beautiful view isn't it?" Casper asked.

I nodded my head. Casper wrapped one arm around me. He used his other hand to point toward the ocean. "You see the light over there. That's the lighthouse on Catalina Island."

"Why don't we go there next weekend?" I asked as I looked into his eyes.

"Don't play with me."

"I'm serious."

"I'll hold you to it."

"Please do," I said as I pressed my body into his.

I felt protected whenever I was in his arms. I took advantage of the moonlit night and we stood stuck in time gazing out into nowhere as the light from the moon bounced off the ocean.

"There you are," I heard Carmen say.

Casper and I turned around and faced Carmen and Xavier. "We aren't the ones who were hiding," I said.

Carmen came and looped her arm in mine. "I was introducing Xavier to some people and you know how I like to talk."

"Yada yada." I held my hand up in protest.

Xavier was excited. "Man, you never told me that Jeanna Fontaine was on drugs."

Casper looked irritated. I could tell he hated that we were interrupted. He blurted out, "I don't go around spreading people's business."

"But still—Jeanna Fontaine. I never would have guessed."

"See, I told you men gossip more than women," Carmen snickered.

"I don't know about y'all, but I'm ready to go," I said, with my Louisiana accent slipping out.

"Xavier, why don't you take the women out front and I'll meet you there shortly," Casper dictated.

Xavier held out both arms. Carmen looped her arm through his left, and I his right. "I'm about to show these cats in Cali how we do it in the south," Xavier proudly said.

I looked at Casper and we both burst out laughing. I don't know where Casper went, but he walked back into the party as we made our way to the front door.

By now we're all sitting in the limousine, minus Casper.

"What's taking him so long?" Carmen sounded irritated.

Carmen was practically sitting in Xavier's lap. He had one of his hands on her knee. Xavier said, "I'll go check. You ladies wait right here."

When he exited the limousine, I asked, "So what's up with Xavier?"

Carmen removed her makeup mirror and freshened up her makeup as we talked. "Nothing. He's a cutie and a lot of fun."

"Don't go breaking his heart." I twirled my curls around my finger. I looked out the window, but there was no sign of Casper or Xavier.

"Girl, please. He's an old player and I'm not the one to get caught."

She protested too much, so I could tell she was smitten with him. "Be careful is all I have to say."

She snapped the mirror shut. "I got it all under control."

* * *

"I've heard that line before."

Carmen moved and sat next to me. She opened up the bar and grabbed a bottle of water. "Would you like one?"

I shook my head.

The door opened up. Casper entered first and sat by me. Xavier sat across from us.

"It's about time." Carmen reached over me and playfully hit Casper.

"Sorry about that ladies. I was cornered by two record execs. Thanks to my brother, I was able to get away."

Before the limousine pulled away, Carmen made sure she was sitting next to Xavier.

"Where to ladies?" Casper asked as he wrapped his arm around my shoulder.

"I'm ready to go home," I said, before leaning into his chest.

The ride over was unusually quiet. We were like two couples engrossed only in their companion. The comfort of lying on Casper's chest made me forget my problems. Casper's whole persona was attractive to me. In a short period of time, Casper had made a major impact on my life. I looked forward to our trip to Catalina Island. I closed my eyes and was awakened when we pulled up in the driveway. The driver opened the door.

"This is becoming a habit." I yawned.

"I love watching you sleep," Casper said.

Xavier teased, "It does nothing for me."

We exited the limousine.

"Parris, welcome to the family." Xavier hugged me

I opened my mouth to respond, but decided n

Seemed like Xavier was tipsy and I wasn't going to entertain him.

Carmen hugged me. "Thanks for a good time."

"Why don't you stay the night?" I asked.

"I sort of have other plans," she said, as she looked at Xavier.

"Don't tell me . . ."

"Don't ask and I won't tell," Carmen stated as she walked toward her car. Xavier followed her.

I stood there with my mouth hanging open.

"Everything okay?" Casper asked.

"Ask your brother," I snapped, before walking toward my front door.

"Wait." Casper had to walk fast to catch up with me. "What's wrong?"

"Nothing," I responded.

He stood in front of me, blocking my path. "I thought we had a nice time."

"We did and apparently so did they." I turned in the direction of where Carmen was parked. They waved as she pulled out of the driveway.

"They're grown. What they do is between them," Casper didn't hesitate to say.

"I don't like it."

He pulled me into his arms. "Why? Because you don't have the guts to do it."

"Move out of my way." I pushed him.

Before I could get the keys in the door, Casper was by my side. "Parris, I'm sorry. If it bothers you that much, why don't you call and check on her when you think she's home."

"Uh. Whatever."

I couldn't get the key in the door. He took the keys and opened the door. "My brother may be a lot of things, but he won't do anything she doesn't want him to do."

He opened the door and walked away. I wanted to call out to him, but didn't. He didn't turn around. I watched him get in the limousine. I closed the door feeling like I was Cinderella who stayed at the ball way past midnight. As I went to turn the alarm off, I asked myself, "How could a wonderful night end on such a sour note?"

I was turning off the downstairs lights when the doorbell rang. By now I had taken off my shoes and was dangling them in one hand. *Carmen must have forgotten something,* I thought.

When I looked through the peephole, I was surprised to see Casper standing there. I opened the door and before words were exchanged, we embraced. I opened my eyes and noticed the limousine pulling away. We walked in and he closed the door. He was the first to speak, "Can I stay the night?"

Without hesitating, I responded, "I thought you'd never ask."

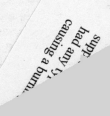

13

THESE ARMS
OF MINE

With my shoes in one hand, I grabbed Casper's hand and led him upstairs. Before I could turn around, he had scooped me up. The shoes dropped to the floor. He placed me on the bed and sat next to me.

"Are you sure?" he asked.

I pulled him toward me. "Ask me in the morning."

He paused. "I don't want to ruin what we have if you're not sure, Parris."

I placed my hand around his head and pulled his lips to mine. With each kiss, I took my tongue and twirled it in his mouth. I pulled away. "Does that answer your question?"

His lips traced their way down my neck. I tried to ~~ss a moan, but failed. It had been so long since I~~ ~~e of intimacy. The feel of his kisses were~~ ~~g desire within. His free hand cupped~~

one of my breasts and my nipples became erect.
Casper's moans could be heard between mine. I wanted
to move, but couldn't. I allowed him to use my body as
his musical instrument. He played my body like a well-
trained pianist. With each touch, he hit the right key.
Before long, we were both naked.

"I love you Parris," he said, before entering me.

Time stopped for me at that moment. I had never
experienced a union such as this. His instrument was
a perfect fit. With each stroke, I was brought to the
brink. Before long, I could no longer suppress it and
in unison we reached a high octave. Neither one of us
could move. We laid on top of the covers as he placed
his head across my chest and held me tight. The next
sound I heard was his snoring. I couldn't complain. He
was right here where I wanted him to be, wrapped up
in these arms of mine.

When I woke up, we were in the same position. I
didn't want to move, but my bladder wouldn't allow
me to lie there. I removed Casper's arms from around
me and slipped out of bed. After using the bathroom,
I decided to take a shower.

Casper was sitting up in bed with the covers wrapped
around his waist when I walked out of the bathroom.
Although a towel was wrapped around my body, under
his gaze, I felt naked. The towel fell some and I pulled
it tighter. "Don't. You have a great body," he said.

"I didn't mean to wake you," I said as I went
through my dresser drawers and found matching peach
underwear.

"The moment I didn't feel your body heat I woke up."

I walked to my closet to put on my clothes. I said, "There're some towels laying on the counter for you."

"Do you have an extra toothbrush I can borrow?" Casper asked.

I could tell he had gotten out of the bed because of the reflection from his voice.

"I'll bring you one," I yelled.

I heard the bathroom door close. My body was still sensitive from our night of lovemaking. It felt good, but I craved to feel Casper's touch. As much as I tried to block the feeling out by finding something to wear, the more my body betrayed me.

I pulled on a purple floral springtime dress and threw on a pair of flat sandals.

My hair had a mind of its own. It was all over my head. I brushed my hair and pulled it back into a pony-tail with a few strands cascading from the side. I knocked on the door of the bathroom, but didn't get an answer. I assumed Casper was still in the shower, but he stood naked in front of the shower at attention when I opened the door.

"I'm so sorry." I blushed.

He didn't seem embarrassed. He continued to dry himself off. "No problem."

I turned to close the door. "Don't," he demanded.

I stood and watched him dry off. Desire for Casper soaked through all pores as my palms and forehead sweated. I wiped the sweat with a towel and located a toothbrush still in the package and handed it to him.

"I'll go cook breakfast," I said, as I rushed from the bathroom. Once outside the door, I sighed.

* * *

Casper came into the kitchen as I was scrambling eggs. To my relief he was fully dressed. My resistance level was nil and there's no telling what I would have done if he hadn't been.

"Something smells good," he said as he wrapped his arms around my waist. He placed a few kisses on the nape of my neck.

"If you don't stop, it won't be fit to eat." I playfully moved him away.

He picked up a slice of bacon from the plate. "This is good."

"I know. Now get out of my kitchen." I popped his hand.

"Ouch."

"A sister don't play when it comes to her food."

With a boyish grin, he said, "I see. I'll be in the living room."

He was making himself feel at home. I was glad.

"Breakfast is ready," I yelled from the living room entranceway.

He turned the TV off and walked my way. "Good, because I've worked up an appetite." He winked.

For a more intimate setting, I decided to use the kitchen table to serve breakfast instead of my formal dining room. Casper pulled my chair out for me before sitting down.

We took turns handing each other plates. From the look of his plate, he wasn't lying when he said he was hungry. He piled on a heaping amount of biscuits, bacon, scrambled eggs, and grits onto his plate. The butter shined on his biscuits and grits.

I poured us each a glass of freshly squeezed orange juice, courtesy of my juice maker.

This time it didn't feel awkward as we ate in silence. When we caught each other looking at the other, we would smile. After drinking the last drop of orange juice, I poured another glass. I glanced at his plate and it was empty. I said, "If you're not full, I can make something else."

He rubbed his stomach. "I couldn't eat another bite. As we say in the South, you put your foot in this girl."

We laughed. I started picking up the dishes and he stood up to help. He said, "Remember, whoever doesn't cook, has to wash." He winked his right eye.

"You won't get an argument out of me." I showed him the location of everything.

The phone rang. I looked at the caller ID and it was Carmen's cell phone. I picked up the cordless phone and started walking into another room.

"Xavier and I were wondering if you had heard from Casper. We're at his place and Xavier doesn't have a key."

Although Casper and I had taken our relationship to another level, I was not ready to share it with anyone. Under the circumstances, I didn't have a choice. "Hold on," I said, as I walked back in the kitchen. I hit the mute button on the phone. "Casper, Xavier doesn't have a key to get in and they're at your place."

I handed him the phone. From what I gathered from his end of the conversation, they would both drop by here and I would later take them both home.

I smiled and said, "I didn't expect company, but we might as well make a day of it. What time is Xavier's plane leaving?"

"I have to drop him off in the morning."

I dialed Carmen's cell. "Carmen, we can have an impromptu barbecue if you guys are up to it."

She repeated what I said to Xavier before responding. "He said he's game. We'll see you shortly."

I hung up with her and looked at Casper and said, "I hope you know how to barbecue."

He held his hand to his chest as if he was offended and said, "All I need is some charcoal and meat and I'll have you slapping your mama by the time I finish."

"Oh really now. Well the charcoal and grill are in the storage area out back. You can set up everything back there."

Before giving him a chance to say anything, I added, "I need to call and have some meat and other food items delivered. I'll be back."

The barbecue was a success. I could tell Carmen and Xavier had more going on than a night between the sheets. The chemistry between the two was undeniable. Casper seemed happy and had made himself at home. He showed Xavier around as if he lived there.

I wasn't able to talk to Carmen about Xavier or about what had transpired between Casper and I. Knowing Carmen, she was dying inside, because she didn't have the details. Carmen agreed to take Casper and Xavier home. I insisted they leave and I would take care of cleaning up the kitchen. I needed time to clear my head and cleaning helped do that.

The entire weekend was unforgettable. It would be something to reminisce about for a while. After making sure everything was secure downstairs, I went upstairs to the master bathroom. I poured some aromatherapy bath salt into the tub and watched the bubbles form. Once I had entered the tub, I hit the whirlpool button and let the water work its magic on my body. I closed my eyes and pretended Casper was sharing this moment with me.

My eyes snapped open because my body reacted to the memory of Casper's kisses and touch. I dried off and wrapped by body in a white terry cloth robe. The warmth of the robe reminded me of how I felt when Casper was wrapped in my arms. Everything at this point reminded me of Casper. I picked up a romance novel and the hero reminded me of him. I was losing the battle, so I called it quits. I turned off the lamp on the nightstand, got under the covers and went to sleep.

14

I'M A FLIRT

"Lance, it's good to see you," I said, after giving him a tight hug. Rose had every right to keep a tight leash on him, because Lance was a handsome man. What she doesn't know is Lance and I had every opportunity to hook up but decided not to years ago.

"Thanks for doing this," Rose said as she sashayed into the room.

We gave each other air kisses. "I wouldn't miss this for the world," I said, noticing the fake smile on Rose's face.

I heard a baby cry from a monitor sitting on the mantle. "I'll be right back," Rose said.

"Junior is teething, so he keeps us running," Lance looked my way and said.

I don't have kids so I couldn't help him in that department. I changed the subject. "I'm sure you heard by now I'll be working with Casper on my next CD."

"Good choice. Although I admit, I'm a little jealous."

Lance pretended to be hurt by using his hand to wipe away an invisible tear.

I chuckled. "You're so silly. I see you haven't changed."

"CJ's good and we've collaborated on a few things. You're in good hands," he said.

I daydreamed about Casper's hands roaming across my body. I must have had a strange look on my face, because Lance asked, "Are you okay?"

"I'm fine. Just fine," I responded, feeling embarrassed. I continued to say, "What do you have in mind for a song?"

Lance led me into their home studio. "Since the movie is a drama, I was thinking of something slow. In fact, I want you and Rose to do a duet."

I dropped my mouth in disbelief. I looked around to see if Rose was returning and she wasn't. I stated, "No offense, Lance, but when I signed up for this, I thought this was going to be a solo."

"Hear me out," he said, as he picked up a remote and hit the play button.

Music blared. I liked the music, but it still wasn't enough to convince me to do a duet with the drama queen of the West. Lance picked up a sheet of music and handed it to me with the lyrics. I scanned it. I closed my eyes and let the music seep into my soul. I opened up my eyes and began to sing a few bars.

I hated to admit it, but Lance was right. I couldn't pass on the song, regardless of my feelings for his woman. Lance leaned back in his chair and smiled. "So is it a go?" he asked.

I blew out some air and said, "Lance, it's like this . . ."

Before I could finish my statement, Lance looked at me with his puppy-dog eyes and pouted. "Pleeease."

Against my better judgment, I said, "Yes."

He got up and twirled me around. Rose picked that opportunity to walk back into the room. I heard her clear her throat. I turned around and she was carrying their six month old son, Lance Jr.

Lance left me and went to kiss Rose, but she turned her head and his kiss landed on her cheek. "Baby, it's on," he said, oblivious to Rose's attitude. He took Lance Jr. from her arms and played with him.

Rose frowned. I pretended to not care. My attention was back on the lyrics in hand. She wasn't the only one who could be a diva, so she needed to get over herself.

Lance wanted to record the song quickly so he could give it to the movie's music supervisor. We spent the next week going through the vocals. As much as I didn't want to do the duet, it actually turned out pretty good. The movie and song would come out close to my CD release.

"You're not too bad," Rose said, after our last day in the studio.

I ignored her statement because when it came to my singing, I didn't need her validation. She went on to say, "You're really a sweet person."

I cocked my head sideways like the detective from one of my favorite shows, *CSI Miami,* and said, "Thank you. I guess."

We were the only ones left in the studio. Rose added, "I heard so many things and didn't know what to expect."

I held my index finger up. "Rose, you should know better than to believe everything you hear."

"I'm glad you're not like some of the others," Rose said in a low voice.

As a woman, I could read in between the lines. I knew exactly where this conversation was headed. The question to myself was should I go there with Rose. She and I were associates and had never been the best of friends.

"Lance only has eyes for you, so you have nothing to worry about," I said.

She looked down at her sparkling engagement ring, smiled and said, "That he does, but he is a man."

I couldn't believe Rose dropped her guard and allowed me to see her insecurity. Here I was having a pep talk with Ms. Hollywood herself. I pulled my chair closer just in case someone else walked in the room because I didn't want them hearing our conversation. "Women can be scandalous, but as long as you trust him, you'll be all right," I stated.

"Trust is hard, but I do trust him," Rose admitted.

"So why worry? You need to concentrate on your wedding. That way the hoochies will definitely get the message that Lance is off limits," I said.

"You have a point. But you know that'll only entice them more. It's something about a married man," Rose responded.

"I wouldn't know. All I know is Lance is crazy about you, and from the looks of things he got you smitten with him too." I teased.

For the first time since we've known each other, Rose and I had a real conversation without any pretenses. She shared more of her feelings for Lance and I told her about my reservations about Casper. We talked, we giggled and we agreed to meet up for brunch soon.

* * *

While trying to find the key to open the kitchen door, I heard the house phone ringing. I hadn't heard from Casper in a few days, so I rushed to answer anticipating hearing his voice.

"I spoke with Rose and she told me you've wrapped up the song," Carmen said, from the other end of the phone.

In between trying to catch my breath and trying not to show disappointment, I said, "It went smoothly. I think you'll like the final output."

"With my two girls on the cut, I know I will," she responded.

I listened to Carmen go on and on about my upcoming album while I undressed and got ready to take a long hot bath. She spoke about Xavier and before she could change the subject to Casper, I said, "My tub is calling me. I'll chat later." I ended the call and escaped from the world for the next forty-five minutes.

The next morning's headline in the entertainment section read, STARS DUEL IT OUT. I wasn't going to read it until I saw a picture of me and Rose walking from the studio. The picture was taken yesterday because I was wearing my apple-bottom jeans and canary-yellow top. I was livid. Of course the writer of this great article was none other than Sandy Blair.

Sandy was becoming a pain in the rear. For some reason, she felt it was her duty to harass me. A part of me felt sorry for her because apparently she had nothing better to do than to follow me and report about my boring life.

I poured myself a glass of grape juice, sat on the bar stool and read the article. I couldn't do anything but laugh. According to the article, Rose and I argued about who would sing lead. Sandy even had the nerve to insinuate Rose cursed me out about how I flirted with Lance in her face. I admit, I'm a flirt, but Sandy had it all wrong. I picked up the cordless phone and dialed a number.

Before I could say anything, Rose said, "Sandy's a trip."

"That and then some," I responded.

"Let's give her more to write about. Meet me for lunch today at Sparkie's," Rose said.

I laughed. "It's a date."

In our last conversation, I asked Casper for space and he was giving it to me. I didn't think he would take me literally. I knew he was out of town, but I halfway expected him to call me at least once to see how I was doing. Be careful what you ask for is a true statement.

I peeped out of my front window to see if any reporters were outside. At first glance, I didn't notice anyone, but a gleam caught my eye and I noticed someone at the end of the driveway. I closed my curtain and went upstairs to find an outfit to wear. Since I knew all eyes would be on us today, I needed to look good. I went for the casual look, so I put on a pair of white Baby Phat jeans adorned with gold-and-silver beads to show off my curves and matching white low-cut jeweled shirt to show off my firm breasts.

Cameras were flashing as soon as I pulled out of my driveway onto the street from my house. I didn't care. I hit the PLAY button on my stereo system and cruised to Sparkie's. Rose was infamous for being late. I valet-parked my car and didn't expect to find Rose seated. The maître d' showed me to our table.

Rose stood and we air kissed. It looked as if we consulted each other on our dress attire, because Rose wore a pair of black Baby Phat jeans with floral designs on the side and matching top. I removed my shades as I sat down.

"All eyes are on us," Rose stated, as she motioned with the movement of her head.

I pretended to be getting something out of my purse and looked in the direction she mentioned and saw Sandy attempting to hide herself behind a menu. Rose and I laughed and talked over our meal. While waiting on the check, her cell phone rang. While she talked, I surveyed the rest of the room. I scanned the dessert menu waiting on Rose to end her call. She looked a little upset.

"What's wrong?" I asked.

"It's Lance Jr. Our nanny is away and Lance doesn't know why Junior won't stop crying. I'm worried it's more than him teething," Rose stated.

Concerned, I said, "If you need to go, I understand."

"This mothering thing is all new to me," she said, while pulling out some money to pay the bill.

I picked up the money and gave it back to her. "This one's on me."

Rose stood to leave and I hugged her. I turned toward Sandy and her cameraman and smiled. "Now run that in tomorrow's paper," I said to myself.

15

WHAT'S MY NAME?

Rose and I laughed when we saw the next day's caption in the paper. WHAT'S REALLY GOING ON? The article mentioned that we came to a truce for the sake of the movie soundtrack and had lunch to seal the deal.

"Sandy's a trip. I wish I knew a desperate man to keep her occupied," I said.

"I wouldn't wish her on my worst enemy, and believe me I have plenty of those," Rose joked.

"You're right. Enough talk about her. How's that beautiful baby of yours?" I asked.

"Lance is Lance," Rose responded.

"I'm talking about Junior," I stated.

Rose laughed. "Oh, my bad. The doctor said the same thing my mom said. He's teething and I don't have anything to worry about."

"I know you're relieved," I responded.

Lance Jr. could be heard in the background crying.

"There he goes. Lance says I spoil him, but I can't stand to hear him cry."

I listened to her go on and on about Lance Jr. while she comforted him. I was about to end the call when she asked, "Will you sing at our wedding?"

A few months ago, I never would have fathomed getting this request from her. I paused before responding. "If there aren't any conflicts, I'll be happy to."

"We're still working out the details, but as soon as we get a date, I'll let you know," Rose said.

The conversation ended shortly thereafter. I spent the day working on the songs for my CD. Thoughts of Casper haunted me through the day and into the night. Although Casper and I weren't a couple, my body craved him. Every time I heard a love song, I thought of him. Every time I read about a hero in one of my romance novels, I thought of him. Casper was taking over my psyche. I needed to get a grip because we had an album to complete. In order to do that, I had to stay focused.

Like LL would say, "Don't call it a comeback." I haven't gone anywhere, but from reading the message boards online, people were talking like I had. The buzz around my upcoming CD kept me motivated and nervous. I fantasized about being back onstage. The marquee flashed the words SOLD OUT. The crowd shouted, "Parris! Parris!" I went out for one, two, three encores. The alarm clock sounded and woke me out of my sleep.

Another night without hearing from Casper had me concerned. We had an album to finish, so I could have called him, but refused to. He knew my number and from what he told me, he should have been back in town by now. His actions confused me. From where I stood, it looked like he was having second thoughts about us. Which is fine, but I needed him to finish my CD.

Once the CD was completed, I wouldn't have to see Casper Johnson again. The thought of it made my stomach turn. I didn't want to imagine not seeing his warm inviting smile or the feel of his hand on the small of my back when he walked me to the car. I didn't want to imagine my life without Casper period, so why hadn't he called me?

It didn't take long to find out the answer to my question. The morning paper's entertainment section showed a picture of Casper and Hailey Barnes, ex-supermodel turned talk show host and the queen of divas with an attitude, seated a little too closely for my tastes at Papa Don's, a new seafood restaurant in the Hills.

Tears flowed from my eyes before I could get a grip on my emotions. "How could you?" I yelled. I threw the paper on the counter. I went to the sink and splashed water on my face. I couldn't get the paper towel off the rack quick enough.

The house phone rang and Casper's name displayed across the caller ID. "Now he wants to call," I blurted. I continued to say, "Since he wants to play games, I'll show him how it's done."

My cell phone rang and I knew it was Casper without looking at the display. I'm not an actor, but with all of the skills I could muster, I answered in a cheerful voice. "Hello there."

"You all right?" he asked.

By now I'm in my living room, so I plopped down on the sofa. "I'm fine. Why wouldn't I be?" I asked.

"No reason. Can I come over? I needed to talk to you about something," Casper said.

I placed my hand over the mouthpiece of the phone and pretended someone else was there. "I have company. I'll call you back."

He said something, but I couldn't make out what it was because I was too busy trying to hang up the phone.

A few hours later, Casper stood outside my front door. I looked a hot mess, so I made him wait until I felt like I was presentable. In fact, I threw on a robe to make it look like I just got out of bed and sprayed on some body mist to give me that "after sex" glow.

"Did I catch you at a bad time?" he asked, when he saw me standing in the doorway in my red satin robe.

I motioned for him to come in. "No. Come on in."

He walked through the door and hugged me. I didn't hug him back. He felt my body tense and pulled away. "You miss me," he said, a sorry attempt to break the ice.

"I was too busy to miss you." I lied. I walked toward the living room with him behind me.

He scooped me up in his arms from behind. "Oh, really now," he said. He planted kisses on the back of my neck.

I managed to squirm out of his grasp. "Not now, Arch," I blurted out.

He asked in a firm voice, "What's my name?"

I turned around to face him. If looks could kill, I would be laid out on a stretcher. "Casper, what's your problem?"

"You just called me another man's name. I can't believe this. I came all the way over here to explain to you about a picture and you're . . ."

I didn't let him finish. "A picture says a thousand

words, but I only have one word for you." I pointed towards the door. "Leave."

He looked at me and opened his mouth to speak, but didn't. He shook his head and stormed out. I slammed the door behind him. The picture on the wall tilted. I cried. My attempt to make him jealous may have backfired. *Wait a minute,* I thought. *What am I doing? He's the one burning the midnight oil with other people.* He's lucky that's all I did. I should have slapped him for coming to me like nothing happened. Another Archie I did not need.

I ignored all of Casper's calls. I knew we had a CD to finish, but I needed some alone time. From listening to his messages, he thought I was having some diva moments and threatened to pull out of our deal. Carmen called me pleading on Casper's behalf. "Dear, you got to get over whatever it is and get back in the studio."

"Casper will be all right," I said, as I enjoyed my spa pedicure.

"He will, but the record company is expecting a CD and if you don't watch it, you're going to be stuck."

"We have enough songs. If he wants to walk, let him walk."

"You got it bad," Carmen stated, as she switched from agent to friend role in seconds.

I felt relaxed for the first time in days. "Put the pink on."

"Excuse me," Carmen said.

"I'm getting my nails and feet done," I responded.

"You need to get your butt to the studio and stop tripping."

"There's a bad connection. I can't hear you," I said, right before clicking the phone off.

I ignored Carmen's other calls.

* * *

"We're ready for your massage now, Ms. Mitchell," the spa receptionist said.

I spent the rest of my afternoon enjoying a Swedish massage. When I left the spa, I felt renewed and ready to tackle the two Cs—Carmen and Casper.

"It's about time," Casper said, when he saw me walk through the doors to the studio.

I rolled my eyes. "Hi, Peter," I said, ignoring Casper altogether.

Peter waved and went back to working the boards. Casper stood up and grabbed my arm. "Ouch," I said.

"Sorry." He loosened his grip as he led me to the other side of the room.

"What's your problem?" I asked, upset he thought he could manhandle me.

"You're my problem," he said, right before leaning down and kissing me.

The moments our lips touched, my mouth betrayed me and opened as his tongue probed around. Our tongues tangoed and dipped as moans slipped out between the two of us. Before it could go further, Casper pulled away. "Now can we get back to the studio and finish recording?" he asked.

He didn't give me a chance to respond. He left me standing there. My eyes followed him as he walked back into the booth. He leaned down and I heard his voice come over the intercom. "Any day now," Casper said.

I took a few deep breaths. I wanted to run and not look back, but my career was in jeopardy and not even

Casper and his arrogance was going to ruin that. I picked up some bottled water on the stand and removed a pill from my purse. I gulped it down, held my head up high and went into the booth to record.

"Parris, that was great. We can wrap it up now," Casper said, as he worked magic on the boards.

I watched him do his thing. Peter looked up and caught me staring. He waved at me as he left the room. My eyes locked with Casper's. I turned away. As I picked up my purse and keys to leave, Casper stood and blocked the doorway. He said, "We need to talk."

"If it's not about my CD, we have nothing to talk about," I responded. By now, I'm attempting to walk around him.

"I'll let you win this battle, but it's far from over," he said, as he moved and allowed me to walk by.

"It never got started," I said, as I twisted away to the elevator.

The elevator door was almost closed when Casper put his hand in the doorway to stop it. He hopped on the elevator. It was the longest elevator ride I had ever had in my life.

16

HE'S MINE

I wasn't home a good five minutes before I heard the doorbell ring. I looked through the peephole and stared at the back of Casper's head. I opened the door and said, "What are you doing here?"

He didn't wait for an invitation, instead, he walked past me into the foyer. "I'm not going another night without us talking."

I closed the door and leaned on it for support. I crossed my arms. "Talk. I'm listening."

"Why did you call me another man's name?"

My eyes opened and closed a few times. "What are you talking about?"

"The other night you called me Arch. You're not over him are you?" he asked.

I started to laugh but the serious expression on Casper's face erased the smile from my face. "Your actions reminded me of him. It was an honest mistake," I responded.

"So I'm having to pay for another man's mistakes?"

By now I'm heated. I recalled seeing him snuggled up with Hailey. "The mistake you made was leading me on."

He walked toward me and reached out to hug me. I moved before he could touch me. "I've never led you on," Casper said.

"A picture says a thousand words that a phone call didn't," I said, as I walked to the living room with him following behind me.

I picked up a copy of the paper with his and Hailey's picture and threw it at him.

"Par—" he said.

"Save it for someone who cares," I interrupted.

"You're not being fair," Casper said.

By now I'm livid. "Fair is not calling me for days. Fair is me seeing you hugged up with some other woman when you said you were into me. Fair is me believing that you weren't up to your playboy ways."

Tears flowed down my face as I continued to lash out at him. Casper allowed me to continue on my rant. When he hugged me, this time I didn't push him away. "Baby, I'm sorry. We ran into each other at the airport. It was nothing but dinner between friends. Nothing more."

We spent the rest of the afternoon talking. He seemed sincere with his apology, but the scene seemed too familiar. Archie used to do and say similar things after being caught. I allowed myself to believe the lie for a moment. I pretended that Casper was the man he proclaimed to be and that I had his devoted attention. Seeing the picture was a reality check.

I was falling for Casper, but I loved myself more. I would not allow him or any other man to mess with my happiness again. I believed Archie's lies, but I refused to be a fool twice in one lifetime. If Casper wanted to pretend all was well, I would go along with the program until my CD was completed. Completing my CD was the most important thing to me at this point, at least that's what I told myself.

"I'm glad y'all kissed and made up," Carmen said, as she passed me a packet of sugar for my hot raspberry tea.

"For now anyway," I said.

Carmen ignored my comments and changed the subject. "Rose tells me you're singing in her wedding."

I sipped my tea after making sure it wasn't too hot. "I'm waiting to hear on the date to confirm for sure."

"She's excited. She can't talk about anything else."

As much as I hated to admit it, Rose wasn't as bad as everyone made her out to be. "You were right. Rose could be fun if you get to know her," I said, in between sips.

"The stunt you two pulled with Sandy was hilarious," Carmen said.

I recounted the actual events of our lunch. "It was Rose's idea, and I loved it."

"You almost let her win though," Carmen said, changing the subject.

The jovial mood I was in changed. "Casper can see who he wants. We're not in an exclusive relationship."

"But you want more don't you?" Carmen asked.

"My music is my only concern," I lied.

Carmen received an emergency phone call from a client and had to leave. I drank the rest of my tea and ordered a chicken salad to go. I had lost weight but could still stand to lose a few more pounds. I juggled my food and purse and ran into Hailey as I was leaving.

Most women were intimidated by Hailey's model-thin figure. She's only a few years younger than I am, but being in her presence made me feel ten years older and ten pounds heavier.

"Parris, we need to talk," Hailey said, ignoring her handsome companion.

"Call Carmen and she'll set up a time," I responded.

"Casper told me what happened."

By then I had walked away, but when I heard her mention Casper's name I turned around. "Excuse me?"

She rushed over to where I was standing. "Casper and I are only friends."

"I couldn't care less," I said, as I gave the valet my ticket.

"If I didn't care about him, I would let you think whatever, but he doesn't deserve your cold treatment." Hailey stood with one hand on her hip.

"What goes on between me and Casper is our business," I said, as I waited on my car.

She leaned in closer. "Don't lose a good man because you're insecure." Hailey flipped her long black curly hair over her shoulders and walked away.

"Ma'am, here's your car," the valet said, as I stared at Hailey as she waltzed away.

I got in my car to leave and to my dismay saw Sandy talking to the valet as I got ready to pull off. I threw my hands in the air and said, "Why me?"

Carmen called me later that night to tell me to turn on the entertainment network news station. I turned the volume up when I saw pictures of me and Hailey standing outside of the restaurant. Sandy glowed as she stuck a microphone in front of the valet's face and he repeated what he thought happened between us. Everybody wanted their one moment of fame. I started to turn it off, but wanted to hear what lie he wanted to tell. The young man said, "And that's when Hailey Barnes said 'He's mine.'"

I clicked off the television. "Carmen, that's bull."

"He's as good as fired," Carmen stated, without me saying another word.

I yelled, "If you're going to report something, at least get the story right."

Carmen ended our call so she could send something to the press. She tried to convince me that although the news wasn't favorable, it would help my record sales. The things I had to put up with as a celebrity were wearing thin with me. My phone rang off the hook. I let all of the calls go to my voice mail, including the ones from Casper.

"You can't hide from me forever," Casper said, from the other side of my front door.

I yelled, "Go away."

"There're reporters outside that would love to hear our conversation, so please let me in."

I peeped through the window and saw the small crowd of folks camped out at the end of my driveway. I unlocked the door and let him in.

"You look terrible," he stated.

I ran my hands through my hair. Rolling my eyes, I replied, "Thanks."

Casper didn't wait for an invitation. He pulled me into a tight embrace. I could hear his heartbeat. Our heartbeats were in sync. "Baby, we'll get through this," he said.

By now, I've pulled myself together. I removed his arms. "There's no we."

"There will always be a we," Casper stated, as he pulled me back into his arms and into a lip-locking session.

When I finally came up for air, I said, "Hailey's a pest, but she's a good person."

I could feel his body release tension. "She wanted to call you and set things straight after the picture came out, but I wouldn't let her."

I held his hand and led him to the couch. "I don't know what to say." Casper wasn't guilty this time. I felt relieved but would still keep my guard up.

"You could say you trusted me," he stated firmly.

I couldn't look him in the eye. I snuggled my body closer to his as we sat on the couch and responded, "I trust you."

"That's what your mouth says." Casper took the remote and turned the stereo on. My CD blasted from the speakers.

I changed the subject. "I hope the guy who did the interview has another job lined up."

"So Hailey told you?"

"Told me what?" I leaned back so I could look him in his face.

"She called the owner and asked that he be fired," Casper responded.

I laughed. "Carmen did the same thing."

"He'll think twice the next time he gets on the TV and tells lies," Casper stated as I laid my head on his chest.

We sat on the couch and listened to music. My reservations were put to rest for now. Our conversation was kept at a minimum but there was no denying the love I was feeling. I wanted to express it to him in more ways than one. I would let him make the next move. Our relationship had been on a roller-coaster ride from the beginning. With my past and nosy reporters, it's a wonder we were even at this point.

Before falling asleep, I recalled saying to myself, "Casper's mine. All mine."

17

ALL FOR YOU

The next few weeks Casper and I were inseparable. He was either at my place or I was at his. We agreed to do most of the recordings using the production company's studio. Otherwise the distraction of being in the privacy of his home would be too much.

Our relationship was new and I enjoyed every minute of it. I got a chance to meet more of his friends and he introduced me as his lady. It felt uncomfortable at first, because we had never really discussed the dynamics of our relationship. People began to recognize us as a couple more and more. The only downside was the heartless comments the media spurred in print and on the entertainment shows. They acted like our five-year age difference was twenty. Casper was far from being naïve, and contrary to their commentary, I was not sleeping with him to revive my career.

I scratched my head as I tried to think of the last

stanza for what would end up being one of the last
songs for the CD. I had blocked out everything else
and didn't notice I wasn't alone. I closed my eyes and
began singing, "You don't have to be lonely . . . Only
if you want to be . . . You don't have to be lonely . . .
You can just call me . . ."

Peter clapped. "I like it."

I turned around. "Peter."

"I didn't want to interrupt you. You were sounding
so good."

I closed my notebook. "You're not just saying that
are you?"

Peter sat in the chair opposite me. "I don't know
why you doubt yourself."

My cell phone vibrated. I opened it up.

"Glad I caught you," Carmen said, from the other end.

I swiveled the chair so that my back was turned to
Peter. "What's up?"

"I need you to do an interview for Black Essence TV."

"No problem, just tell me when," I responded.

"Today."

"What? I'm looking like I just got out of bed." I
hopped out of the chair and walked to the full-length
mirror.

Peter commented. "You look fine to me."

"Stay out of this Peter." I turned around.

He held his hands up. "Just speaking the truth, my
dear," he stated.

"I know this is last minute, but I got you on as a performer with the condition I would give them an exclusive interview," Carmen said, without breathing once.

I'm fuming. I hated surprises and being put on the
spot. I was beginning to feel like I was a puppet playing
somebody else's game. I momentarily forgot Carmen

was a friend. Right now she was acting as my agent on the thin line between agent and friend. "I'm not ready to go back on stage. It's been two years and I don't have a band . . . dancers . . . what were you thinking?"

Carmen tried to calm me down. "I have it covered. The band members you used before were ecstatic about going back on stage with you."

"You've thought of everything, but why am I the last one to know?" By now my blood pressure had lowered.

Peter shook his head. He knew not to interrupt me again.

"You've been making progress in the studio and didn't need to be bothered with minor details," she said.

I addressed Peter. "Can you call Casper and ask him to meet me at my place?"

"Sure." Without getting up, Peter moved his chair to the phone at the other end of the console.

"Carmen, I want to wring your neck right now. Have the reporter meet me at my house around six this evening." I hung the phone up.

I knew Carmen was only looking out for my best interest, but it didn't stop me from being mad at her. Doing the interview and performing at the BEAM awards would be an opportunity to promote my upcoming CD and once I speak with Casper, it might be the opportunity for me to release a single. It'll be sooner than planned, but if anybody could make it happen, I knew Casper could.

"I owe you one," I said, before giving Peter a quick hug.

* * *

Casper was waiting outside my house in his car talking on his cell phone when I pulled up. I heard him say, "I need it done *now*."

One thing I can say about Casper. He doesn't play around when it comes to business. He's the sweetest guy you ever want to meet, but don't try to mess over him. He got out of his SUV and hugged me, but his headpiece was still glued to his ear and he was still talking. He followed me inside.

He soon ended his call and said, "Sorry about that. I'm trying to get my assistant on the east coast to take care of something."

I held my hand up. "Handle your business." I opened the refrigerator. "Would you like something to drink or eat?"

With desire beaming from his eyes, he said, "I would, but it can't be found in your refrigerator."

I blushed. "Under normal circumstances, I would oblige, but I have a situation."

"Anything I can do to help?"

He passed me a glass out of the cabinet. I poured myself a glass of grape juice. "Actually there is."

"Name it and it's done."

I took small sips from the glass before stating, "We need to decide on which song we're going to release as a single, because I'm supposed to perform at the BEAM awards."

I couldn't tell how he felt, because his face was emotionless. He rubbed his chin; something he often did whenever he was in deep thought. I stood and waited for a response. He said, "Don't worry. We can do this."

I walked over to him and wrapped my arms around his waist. "Thank you, Sweetie."

"The hardest part is deciding on which song to release first."

"I know. I came up with some lyrics to that track you gave me. I think it should be the first single."

Back in business mode, Casper said, "I'll give you my opinion after I hear it."

I squeezed him tight. "It's a deal."

"Why don't we go upstairs and seal it?" he asked.

I dropped my arms to my side. "Can't. I need to be showered and dressed for an interview. Black Essence should be here in about two hours."

"I didn't know you had an interview," he stated.

"I only found out about an hour ago," I responded.

"Let me get out of your hair. I know how you value your privacy, so I don't want to give them any reason to ask you questions about us." I could sense sarcasm in his voice.

"A month ago, I would have had a problem with it. But I'm secure enough in our relationship to know where we stand with each other."

Casper smiled. "I'm so happy to hear that."

I walked Casper to the door. Before leaving, he kissed me. "I love you. Call me later."

"I love you too," I said for the first time. Casper stopped in midstep.

He turned around. "Did I hear you correctly?"

"Yes."

He walked back toward me. "Say it again."

"I love you."

"She loves me." He picked me up and twirled me around.

We kissed again.

"You better get going or the interviewer will catch us both in our birthday suits." I joked.

"Baby, right now, I don't even care."

I gave him a "don't go there" look, so he backed down. "I can take a hint," he said, sounding like a reprimanded child. He continued to say, "Call me as soon as they leave."

We sealed it with a kiss. When he reached his car, he yelled, "Say it one more time."

"I love you, silly. Bye." I laughed and waved.

I remember the first night we made love, he confessed his love for me, but I couldn't bring myself to admit it to him at the time. I knew some time ago he had my heart, but saying the "I love you" words was an entirely different story. I watched him drive away. I also saw a few flashes. At this point, I didn't care about nosy reporters. I was in love. I repeated it to myself. It felt good to admit it.

When I reentered the house, the clock chimed. Two hours and it'll be show time. Time to give the interviewer a view of the new and improved Parris.

The interview went well. My comeback onto the music scene was making some people antsy. No one knew what to expect. Since my new CD was announced, folks had been trying to get a sample of the music. Casper planned to leak the single on the Internet as soon as we finished.

Casper had given me a garage door opener and keys to his house so I could come and go as I pleased. I could hear music blasting from the studio as I made my way downstairs. He looked up and motioned for me to come behind the booth.

He stood up and kissed me. "Baby, you're right. I

listened to the CD you made. I've been working on the track. All I need is your beautiful voice."

I didn't want to be released from his arms, but I knew we had a long night ahead of us. My career was riding on this. I walked into the singing booth, put the headphones on and said, "Let it rip."

He played the music and when he gave me the cue, I started singing.

Hey sexy thang . . .
What's on your mind . . .
You say you're a little lonely . . .
And do I have some time . . .
Anything for you . . .
Tell me whatcha want to do . . .

'Cause you don't have to be lonely . . .
It's only if you want to be . . .
You don't have to be lonely . . .
You can just call me . . .

Just give me a minute and . . .
I'll be on my way . . .
Don't forget to turn the alarm off baby . . .
'Cause I'll be over to stay . . .

You don't have to be lonely . . .
Now that you have me . . .
You don't have to be lonely . . .

It took us a few hours to record the song. We worked together to modify the song arrangement to satisfy us both. By midnight we both agreed that the midtempo song "You Don't Have To Be Lonely" would be the song that would put me back on the map.

We were so excited about it that we made love right there in the studio. It was intense and spontaneous and I loved it. Being with Casper opened me up to a new world of pleasure—in and out of the bedroom.

I woke up in Casper's bed the next morning still groggy from the night before. With eyes still closed, I reached for him and he wasn't there. I turned over to see an imprint of where his body had been. After stretching, I went to the bathroom and washed my face. I admired myself in the mirror. A few months ago, there would have been no way I would walk around naked. Casper made me feel comfortable with my body and encouraged me to be naked not only in the dark, but in the light.

I turned the shower on. I walked out of the bathroom and went to a special section of his closet that I made for myself. I told him if I was going to be at his place, then I would need to have clothes here. After picking out a pair of jeans and a red T-shirt he bought me with the word DIVA printed across the front, I returned to the bathroom. The steam fogged up the mirrors.

By the time I got dressed and exited the bathroom, Casper had made up the bed and had set up a small table in his room with two place settings filled with breakfast. "You did all of this for little old me?" I sniffed the flowers that were placed on the table as a centerpiece before sitting down.

"Everything I do is all for you. I thought you knew that by now," he said, as he held my hand to say grace.

We bowed our heads as he blessed our food. When

he finished, I looked at him and smiled. I felt at peace. "This is good," I said in between bites of my cheese omelet.

We were at a comfort level with one another. This was one of those times we simply enjoyed one another's company. Words were not needed.

18

MY, MY, MY

Carmen sat in her favorite chair in my bedroom flipping through the latest issue of *Noir* magazine. "My, my, my. Love is in the air." She commented.

"Whatever."

"Feisty little thing aren't we?" She joked.

"I'm surprised you have the time to read anything," I said in the most sarcastic voice I could muster. I was packing for a video shoot and was back and forth between my closet and bed with clothes.

"When I got the advanced copy, your interview is the first thing I read."

"I hope you got an eye full."

She fanned herself with the magazine. "You sure you don't need me to come chaperone."

"We have an entire crew of people. So no, Casper and I don't need chaperones," I snapped.

"I told Xavier . . ."

I stopped packing and interrupted and said, "You and Xavier have been blowing up the phone waves a lot."

"We talk every now and then." She looked away.

"According to a reliable source, you guys talk all of the time." I started packing again and said, "And by the way, that trip you took to Atlanta last month . . ." I wanted to laugh at the expression on Carmen's face. "I know all about it. Not details, but enough to know it wasn't *just* business."

"You need to stay out of grown folks' business."

"When you stay out of mine, I'll stay out of yours." One for me. Zero for Carmen. I chuckled.

She stood up and walked over to the bed. "Let me help you with this."

I laughed. "Oh no my highness, sit back down. I got this." I added, "It doesn't feel good when somebody is all up in your business, now does it?"

Carmen tried her best not to smile. "Don't you have a plane to catch?"

I responded, "It's not going anywhere."

I wasn't going to let Carmen off too easy. I teased her all of the way to the airport.

"I'm glad you chartered a plane," I whispered in Casper's ear. I looked out the window and admired the beauty of the white puffy clouds.

Casper squeezed my hand. I let my seat back, closed my eyes and took a nap. When I woke, he was reading a copy of *Noir* Magazine and smiling. He said, "You are full of surprises."

"I don't know what you mean." I faked amnesia.

"For someone who wanted to keep our relationship

private, you didn't have a problem talking about us." He teased.

"I'm not ashamed to talk about us. Besides, it's not like it's a secret anyway."

"But . . ."

I took my index finger and placed it over his lips. "You're special to me and now the whole world knows."

He began sucking on my fingers. I jerked my hand away. "Casper."

"What did I do?" he asked, batting his eyes like he was innocent.

"There are people around." I looked around at the crew who was flying down with us for the video shoot.

"They're all asleep," he stated.

"Like you should be," I added, before crossing my arms.

"I love it when you pretend to be mad." He pinched my cheek. "You look so cute."

"Go to sleep Casper."

"I love you," he said as he reclined his seat.

It was 7 P.M. Pacific time by the time we landed in the Bahamas. We gathered in several vans to go to our destination—the Atlantis on Paradise Island. It was the first time for some of the crew members. I had been on the island several times and each time I found a new hidden treasure of beauty.

We were treated like royalty when we arrived at the hotel. Casper gave strict orders. He told everyone they had one day for themselves, but the following day we would all need to be up bright and early for an early morning video shoot.

I for one was relieved to have a day to enjoy the island. I don't know what Casper planned on doing tonight, but I wanted to take a walk along the beach. We weren't sharing rooms, but he made sure we had two adjoining suites.

I was putting on a floral wrap, when I heard Casper knock on the door between our suites. "Just a minute," I yelled.

He was dressed in a tropical floral shirt and shorts. Casper could make a plaid suit look good. "That color looks good on you," I managed to say, before he pulled me into his arms and kissed me.

This was our first kiss on the island. When working, we tried to keep our public display of affection down to a minimum. "If you don't stop, we won't make it downstairs," I said, between kisses.

"I don't mind."

I removed myself from his embrace and grabbed his hands. "I do." I grabbed the hotel key and pulled him out the door. "Let's go for a walk on the beach."

"At this time of night?" he responded. He was doing whatever he could to keep me in the room. Although my body craved his, I was determined to enjoy one of my favorite islands.

"This is the best time," I said, pushing him toward the door.

"I forgot something," he said, before heading back to his room.

I walked to the elevator and pushed the down button. If he didn't hurry, he would have to meet me downstairs. When the elevator opened, I saw him running down the hall. "Wait."

Oblivious of the attitude shown on the other passengers faces, I held the door until he made it.

* * *

The place had gotten crowded since we first arrived.
The hotel had a casino and it was full of tourists. The
islanders weren't permitted to gamble, so every "cha-
ching" sound we heard was someone here visiting.

"I love this place." I twirled around when we got
outside.

Before walking toward the beach, I coerced Casper
into walking through the aquarium that was part of the
hotel. I wanted to see if I could recognize any new sea
creatures. We walked through the aquarium, stopping
occasionally to admire the beauty of the different tropical fish. The air outside was crisp. Not a cloud appeared in the sky. An endless amount of stars shined
down on us as we walked hand in hand up what
seemed like an endless stretch of beach.

"Why don't we walk over there?" Casper pointed as
he led me toward a secluded spot.

I was surprised to see a table set up with food from
the island and fresh fruit. A man dressed as a waiter lit
the candles that adorned the table. "Casper." My hand
went up to my mouth.

"Surprise," he said, as he leaned down and kissed me.

"You got me." I was elated.

We dined on fresh mango and other island treats. I
was glowing. Casper had made one of my fantasies a
reality. Although we lived in Los Angeles and had
access to many beaches, nothing could beat being here
on Paradise Island with my man. The sounds resonat-
ing from the waves of the ocean in the background
were music to my ears. We were in a secluded area,
but every now and then a couple would venture out
and I could hear someone say, "Oh, how romantic."

My heart was full. As I sat across from Casper, all I could think about was how special he made me feel. There were times I wanted to wring his neck, but the majority of the time all I wanted to do was love him. He was my missing link. It took me getting control of my life and becoming whole again to find him. That night, I vowed that no matter what, nothing would come between us.

When we were walking down the hallway, I swore I heard a familiar voice. I shrugged it off. Tonight had been perfect and I was not going to let anything spoil it.

"Your place or mine?" Casper asked as he kissed me outside my door.

I responded between kisses, "Tonight mine, and tomorrow yours."

"That's what I like about you. You come up with some good ideas."

I couldn't get the door opened fast enough. We were all over each other. The bed was just a fixture in the room as far as we were concerned. My balcony faced the ocean and before I knew it, we were out on the balcony making love. We tried to cover up each other's sounds with our hands. Between giggles and orgasms, neither one of us would forget our first night together in the Bahamas.

The following day, we met some of the crew for breakfast. Afterward we split up. I wanted to go to the Straw Market and buy a few keepsakes for my mom and friends back at home. Casper needed to check out the location for the video shoot. We agreed to meet up that afternoon back at the hotel.

Sharon Gill, a makeup artist hired for the video shoot, and I went from booth to booth buying up everything in sight. Besides the key chains and post-cards, I purchased some beautiful hand-crafted jew-elry and handbags. I bought Casper and me matching T-shirts. Sharon loaded up on jewelry as well and fabric. If we didn't stop shopping, we would need a truck to carry back all of the things we purchased.

The fun about the whole shopping expedition was bargaining with the merchants. If you accepted the first price they gave you, you were a fool. We were able to talk them down on their prices; however, if the merchants refused to lower their price, we left their shops and went to the next one.

"I don't think I can walk another step," Sharon said.

"I'm hungry," I said, as my stomach growled.

"I saw a quaint restaurant across from here." Sharon attempted to point, but couldn't because of the bags in her hands.

We made our way across the street to the restaurant. After being seated, Sharon and I had a chance to talk. She didn't wear much makeup, but didn't need to. She was a natural beauty. She was in her early twenties and had lucked out on this assignment when my regular makeup artist got sick and was advised not to travel. Sharon left the table to go to the restroom.

Behind me I could hear an annoying, yet familiar voice. I wanted to turn around, but if it was who I thought it was, I don't think I would have been able to stand. I retrieved my makeup mirror from my purse and positioned it so I could see behind me. I gasped. The mirror in my hand fell to the table. I couldn't believe my eyes. It couldn't be. I had to be dreaming. It must be the heat. I'm more exhausted than I realized. I picked up the mirror again and repositioned it. There was no mistake, it was Archie. I assumed the woman sitting directly behind me was Sylvia. I couldn't tell because her hair was now a different color and it could have been a wig.

Sweat started dripping from my forehead. I picked up the napkin and wiped as much as I could. I had a cell phone, but it didn't work over here. I had to notify the authorities. I wanted to confront the two of them, but I knew if I did, they would run and then I would never have the chance to make them pay for what they did to me.

Breathe. Breathe, I kept telling myself.

"Are you okay?" Sharon asked as she slid back into her chair.

I lowered my voice and said, "Yes and no."

She looked confused as I wrote a note instead of verbally responding. She read it and said, "Let's slip out that way."

I left more than enough money to cover our food on the table before we slipped out with bags in tow. "I need to find the authorities and see what rights I have. Do me a favor. Find Casper and tell him where I'm at."

"Maybe we should stick together." Sharon sounded concerned.

I flagged down a taxi. "Here, take these with you." I helped place the bags in the cab. I recalled passing the police station. "I'm walking to the police station. I'll be all right," I reassured her.

As I walked to the police station, men flirted. It was annoying and I wanted to scream. By the time the police were convinced of who I was and the crime

Archie had committed, Archie was no longer in the restaurant. I gave them a good description and directed them to contact the States for a photo. I described what he and his accomplice were wearing.

Casper came and I knew I looked a wreck. He put his arms around me and I wanted to close my eyes and pretend this was all a bad dream. How could a nice trip turn into this? I asked myself.

"Sweetheart, they'll catch him and you can put this all behind you." Casper comforted me as he ran his hands through my hair.

I didn't say a word. The chief of police insisted we return to our hotel. He assured us that they would get word to me immediately if anything developed. An off-duty officer volunteered to drive us back to our hotel.

"Now that I know we're in the same vicinity, it's going to be hard for me to sleep," I told Casper as I laid my head on his chest as we drove through the city.

"They'll find him."

Being pessimistic, I said, "I doubt it. It's a hopeless situation. They're probably long gone by now."

I looked out the window as we passed some of the neighborhoods. It was a shame that one of the prettiest places in the world was subject to the amount of poverty I saw in the area. I made a mental note to do a benefit concert with all proceeds going to benefit the islanders.

19

LOST WITHOUT YOU

I didn't feel like being around people, so Casper ordered room service. Sharon called a few times to check on me, but I didn't return her calls. Casper made sure he notified the crew of what happened to avoid any unnecessary rumors. Everyone was on high alert and wanted to catch Archie almost as much as I did. I was mentally exhausted and fell asleep while Casper stroked my hair. The phone ringing woke us both up.

"Hello," Casper sleepily answered. "Hold on."

He handed me the phone. "Who is it?" I mouthed.

"You'll want to talk to him," he responded.

The chief of police was on the phone. "Ma'am, we need you to come down and make a positive identification."

He explained that it would take a while for them to confirm Archie and Sylvia's fingerprints and without a positive identification, they would not be able to hold them long. I sat straight up in the bed. "You got

him. What about the woman? Did you get her too?" I
blurted out.

"Yes. You can come down in the morning."

"No. I'm coming down now," I interrupted him, as
I threw the covers off.

"We'll send a car to pick you up."

"Thank you. Thank you." I told the officer before
hanging up.

"They got him."

Casper tried to calm me down. "I know dear."

I got up and looked for my shoes. "They need me to
identify them."

"It's three in the morning, why don't we wait until
at least the sun comes out." Casper remained in bed.

"I'm going now. I won't be able to go back to sleep
anyway."

He stretched. "That's true and then you'll keep me
up all night."

"On second thought, I'll take a quick shower. I want
to be fresh for the video shoot."

Casper grudgingly got up. "I've pushed the shoot
back to eight instead of six. That'll give everybody time
to have everything set up by the time we get there."

"I thought you wanted to capture the sunrise."

"One of the cameramen will be set up for it. You
don't need to be there."

I walked to where he was standing and gave him a
tight hug. "You think of everything. I don't know what
I would do without you."

"Let's hope you'll never have to find out." He
kissed the top of my head. "Now, go take that shower.
I didn't want to say anything earlier, but . . ." He joked.

"Don't even go there."

Before he could respond, I was in the bathroom.

* * *

Somebody must have leaked it to the local press, because when we got to the station, the cameras were flashing. A reporter threw a microphone in my face and Casper pushed him away.

"No comment," he yelled.

I couldn't care less about the media at this point. The only thing on my mind was seeing justice served. It was four in the morning and today was the day I saw my worst nightmare end. We were led into a room and shortly the chief of police entered.

He extended his hand. "Ms. Mitchell, I'm sorry your trip was ruined by this scum."

I responded, "So am I."

"Sorry about the cameras too. We haven't had this much media excitement on the island since the Anna situation."

I tuned him out. My eyes were fixated on Archie and Sylvia sitting on the other side of the window. I could see them, but they couldn't see me. The chief turned on a recorder. "Ms. Mitchell, can you identify those two people?"

"Yes. That's Archie Walker." I pointed at Archie. "And Sylvia Walker."

"Thank you."

"What's next?" Casper asked. Not once leaving my side.

"We can hold them until we get the fingerprints back."

"How long will that be?" I couldn't resist asking.

"Any time now. We move a little slower over here." He tried to joke.

I didn't find it funny, but forced myself to smile.

Another officer walked in the room and handed him a file. The chief thumbed through it and smiled, "Well, we got ourselves some international criminals. Not only did they steal from you, but they have been cheating our tourists claiming to be the owners of a resort."

Casper and I sat in disbelief. "And that means?" I blurted.

"It means they will be serving time for a very long time. I have a friend in the States that will be here tomorrow. Don't worry your pretty little head. Justice will be served."

I was relieved, but there was one thing I needed to do. Casper disagreed, but I convinced him and the chief that it would help me sleep better. Casper didn't want me to enter the room alone; although they were still handcuffed and being guarded. "I can do this," I kept telling myself.

The expression on their faces when they saw me was priceless. I couldn't help smiling. I wasn't an actress, but this morning, I was going to be melodramatic. "Well, well. You didn't think you would see me again, now did you?"

Neither said a word. Sylvia rolled her eyes and looked away. Archie stared, his eyes full of venom. "You don't have to say a word. Just listen," I said.

I went on and on about how I survived although he tried to break not only my heart, but my spirit. With each sentence, I got stronger and stronger. I could feel Casper's hand on the center of my back, but what he didn't realize is I now had enough strength to face the man who stole everything from me.

"I'm sorry," Archie said, without looking me in the eyes.

"Maybe if I would have heard those words two years ago, I would have some leniency. Not!" I snapped.

"We were so good together. If you drop the charges, I'll divorce her and I'll do whatever you want to make up. Anything," Archie said.

I couldn't believe this. Archie was trying to use his persuasiveness to get me to come around. A delirious laugh seeped out from within me. "You have to be kidding."

"I never loved her anyway. She was just something to do when you weren't around."

I could see the hurt in Sylvia's eyes. "He had it planned from the moment he saw you. I'm an innocent victim in all of this," Sylvia spoke with vengeance.

"She can talk ladies and gentleman." I held my head back and laughed.

"Parris. I love you. I didn't mean to hurt you," Archie kept saying.

"You did me a favor." I turned to Casper. "I'm ready to go."

Casper didn't say a word. I'm sure he was tripping on the entire scene.

Before leaving the room, I turned around and said, "I owe you both a thank you. If it wasn't for you; I wouldn't be the woman I am today."

As we left the room, I said under my breath, "I hope you both rot in jail."

We left the room and I felt good. Casper didn't say anything until we got back to the hotel. I had to call Carmen to let her know what happened so she wouldn't be surprised. I was too late, because the light was blinking on the hotel phone.

"Yes, Carmen, I'm fine. In fact, I feel G-R-E-A-T," I assured her.

After ending our conversation, I changed my clothes. Before exiting the hotel, I had to give a quick statement to the press. Casper and I snuck out the back of the hotel afterward.

The crew was relieved to find out that Archie was behind bars. We spent the first hour on location answering their questions. Afterward, Casper got us all back on track. "Let's do what we traveled thousands of miles to do."

"I'm so glad it worked out for you," Sharon said as she applied my makeup.

"You and me both," I commented.

She handed me a mirror so I could check out her handiwork. "Perfect," I commented.

I could tell Casper was a little jealous that the actor in the video was getting my attention. I had to admit the actor would make most women drool. But in my eyes, Casper had him beat by at least an inch. I chuckled. Casper didn't have to worry about a thing. What he didn't know was that I had to pretend the actor was him when I sang the lyrics to "You Don't Have To Be Lonely."

It took us all day to film those scenes. I should have been exhausted from the heat and the consta   ap-plying of makeup and wardrobe changes, bu Coming to the Bahamas accomplished n could have ever anticipated.

We were going to shoot a couple of sce Zoo. Casper had worked it out with th was closed down and only the extras would be allowed in. I fanned myself. "It's hot up in here."

"Diva, we'll get you some air," Sharon teased.

The crew was amazed at how easy I was to work with. They swore that some of the singers they worked with were barracudas. I wouldn't agree or disagree. In situations like this, it was best to keep your comments to yourself. People could turn your words into something else and before you knew it, you would be feuding with another artist over words you couldn't remember you said.

The club scene didn't take long to shoot. I was relieved because the heat was killing me. I would rather be out with the sun blazing than closed up in the building. The lights they used didn't help. The fans had to be turned off at one point or risk a power surge.

Casper hired Dion Perkins to direct the video. He was instrumental in seeing that our vision was taken into consideration in the final output. After the last shot, Dion shouted, "It's a wrap."

We all cheered. "Dion, I owe you one," I said as I leaned over and kissed him on the cheek.

"The pleasure has been all mine. When Casper called me about doing it, I was more than thrilled. You were magnificent."

"She sure was," Casper confirmed. "Where's my kiss?" He tried to sound jealous.

"I gave them all away." I teased.

He pulled me into his arms and ignored the glares from the crew. They started cheering. I wiped the lipstick from Casper's lips.

"Let's go. I hear the beach calling me," I said.

"I'm right behind you."

* * *

We strolled along the beach. The warm sand slid between my toes through my open-toed sandals. As a small wave descended on to the beach, Casper stopped and dropped to his knees.

"What are you doing?" I stared down at him.

"I was going to wait. But I don't know when we'll get the opportunity to be alone again."

I hope he wasn't going to do what I thought he was.

He continued to say, "When we get to the states you're going to be so busy getting ready for the BEAM awards performance."

"Uh-huh," is all I was able to say.

"You don't have to give me an answer now. In fact, I want you to think about it for a few days."

He held my hand with one of his and reached into his pocket with the other. He released my hand and took up a four-carat princess-cut sapphire ring surrounded by diamonds.

"I love you more than I ever thought possible. You complete me. I am able to be a better man, just because I have you in my life. I promise to always put you first. I will not do anything to intentionally hurt you. I apologize in advance if my quest to please you causes you any pain. Parris Mitchell, will you do me the honor of being my wife?"

I opened my mouth to speak, but nothing came out.

"Shh. I don't want your answer right now. I want you to be as sure as I am." He slipped the ring on my finger.

I admired it as the diamonds glistened in the moonlight. "Casper, I would be lost without you. I already know my answer."

He stood up and cradled me in his arms.

Because of Casper I would have plenty of good memories to remind me of our trip to Paradise Island. As we walked back to the hotel, I thought about the whole trip; the good, the bad, and the miracle that God had performed in my life. It's a miracle that I'm able to love someone as much as I love Casper. He wanted me to wait and tell him his answer. I knew the perfect time to tell him. I would wait. Wait until we were back in the States.

20

WALL TO WALL

The birds chirping woke me up. I felt safe and secure in Casper's arms. Coming to the Bahamas was just what I needed to close one door and open another. Casper smiled in his sleep. His face looked peaceful. I kissed him on the cheek. He stirred, but didn't wake up. I attempted to remove his arm from around me so I could go take a shower. He moaned.

"Go back to sleep," I said, as I placed the cover back on him. He grabbed the pillow and hugged it in my absence.

I went to my room, showered and changed clothes. When I walked back through the adjourning door, Casper was in the shower. Instead of disturbing him, I left him a note to let him know I would be in the lobby. I picked up the thin prepaid cell phone Casper bought me and my credit card, and placed them in my pocket and headed downstairs.

As I strolled through the indoor mall of the hotel, my

mind felt at peace. I hummed as I went from one shop to the next. I didn't feel like going back to my room to use the bathroom, so I found one in the hotel lobby. While I was washing my hands, I looked in the mirror and saw Sylvia's reflection.

I felt groggy. My head hurt a little and when I opened my eyes, all I could see was black. It was dark because something was covering my eyes. I attempted to talk, but felt something in my mouth. My hands were bound and I couldn't move. My body shook with each bump. It felt like I was in a moving vehicle.

I heard Sylvia's voice, "Looks like your girlfriend's waking up."

Muffled, I asked, "Where am I?"

My mind went haywire. I thought Archie was locked up. Here I am on foreign soil and kidnapped. I couldn't believe this. Would I live or die? Who would tell my mother? Does Casper know I'm missing? A million things went through my mind.

I listened to them go back and forth. I guess their honeymoon was over because they argued most of the way to our destination. When we stopped, I heard the door open. Archie pulled me out and threw me over his shoulder. The stench from his shirt made me want to puke. I could hear leaves break beneath us as he carried me to a destination unknown.

"Put her over there," Sylvia blurted.

He threw me and I yelped when my body hit something. It felt like a couch. Archie removed the scarf covering my eyes. It took a moment for my eyes to adjust. I hoped my eyes wouldn't betray the terror I felt. The smile across Archie's face confirmed that they did.

"You're not talking all that smack now are you?" His sinister laugh sent a chill down my spine.

He removed the sock from around my mouth but kept my arms and feet bound. He sat me up. I coughed. Sylvia walked over with a silver cup. "Drink this," she said.

The cup looked dirty, but I was thirsty and didn't know when I would be offered anything else to drink. I gulped down the water. I stared at them both, afraid to talk.

"Now what Sherlock?" Sylvia asked.

"Shut up so I can think," Archie stated as he rocked back and forth in his chair.

For now, I had to figure out what to do. I didn't know where I was. If I could get out of the house, I would run like my life depended on it. In fact, looking between Archie and Sylvia, it did.

"We could ask for ransom. That'll be enough to get us off the island," Archie stated.

"If you wouldn't have gambled all the money away at the casinos, we would have money," Sylvia snapped.

As they bickered, I scanned the room. I felt a cool draft. I looked down to see holes through the wooden floor. From wall to wall, the panels appeared to be falling apart. With all of the money Archie stole from me, he should have been able to afford more than this shack. I saw two doors. The front door didn't appear to have a lock on it, but was bordered up where a window used to be. I began to sneeze. The room could stand a good dusting.

"I need to pee," I said.

They both turned to look at me. Archie was the first to speak. "Take her out back."

"I'm not her keeper," Sylvia retorted.

"Until I can think of how we're going to get more money, you are," Archie said, before storming out of the room.

"How could you let him punk you like that?" I asked.

"The same way you did," she responded.

Ouch. Sylvia knew exactly what punch to throw. She untied my legs. With her help, I was able to stand. She grabbed the rope around my hands and led me out a set of doors. We were in the back. I saw a teenage boy peeking from around a bush. I mouthed the word "help." Sylvia saw the boy too and pulled me along. I almost fell. I couldn't believe it. People still used outhouses in this day and time.

"I'm not using that," I stated.

"I don't care if you use it, just go," she said.

I looked at her and then at my hands. "How am I supposed to pull down my pants?"

"If you try to escape, I'll shoot you," Sylvia stated in a quiet voice. She pointed to an object in her pocket that could have been a gun. She untied me.

I didn't want to take any chances, so I didn't try her. The cell phone was still in my pocket. During their abduction, they didn't check my pockets. Thank goodness they didn't. Now, I had to see if I could get a signal in what looked like the boondocks.

I held my breath as she opened the door to the outhouse. The funk almost made me pass out. I removed the phone and couldn't get one bar. Casper bought us temporary phones while on the island so it should have worked. I was frantic. "Pull yourself together," I kept telling myself. I squatted down and used the bathroom. I thought I felt something slimy on my leg and jumped out of the outhouse and right into Sylvia.

She went to grab the weapon out of her pocket. "What's your problem?"

I started hitting my legs. "I felt something crawling on my leg," I responded. It was a huge bug that reminded me of a caterpillar. I stomped it with my shoe.

"Come on." She pushed me back towards the house. I looked for the young man, but he was nowhere to be found. I could only hope he heard our conversation and went to get me some help. As we walked back in, an idea hit me. I would wait until Archie was around before bringing it up.

Archie was pacing the floor. Sylvia pushed me on the couch. "Next time you take her out," she snapped. She threw the ropes at Archie. He grabbed one set, but the other hit the floor.

"I have an idea," I said. Neither one responded. I reached into my pocket and held out a credit card. "Why don't we leave this joint and go to nicer quarters?"

Sylvia snatched the card from my hand. She looked it over and handed it to Archie. "I agree," she stated.

"No," Archie responded.

Sylvia looped her arms around Archie. "Baby, it's the least she could do. She owes us for the headache she's caused us." She looked over at me with a half smile.

Archie looked at me too. "You're right. Go pack the rest of our stuff while I tie her up. We won't be coming back to this joint again."

I'm not sure how long it took them to get ready, but before I knew it, I was laid in the backseat of the car with tape around my mouth and a blanket over my body. It was a hundred degrees outside and I was burning up. I tried to tell them I didn't need a blanket, but Archie refused to take the tape off my mouth.

The sun was going down by the time we made it to our destination. I listened as both car doors opened. Shortly thereafter, I heard my door open. Archie sat me up and untied me. "If you say one word, not only will I kill you, but anyone who is in our path." I followed his eyes to the opening of his jacket. Staring back at me was a huge gun.

These two scam artists were really getting over. The hotel Archie chose was more like guest homes. Under normal circumstances, I could see myself vacationing here. Right now, however, all I could think about was a way for me to escape.

Once in the room, Archie tied me to a chair. When he ordered room service, he made sure Sylvia blocked the view so the hotel worker wouldn't be able to see me. I savored the food given to me as if it were my last meal. The last few times I went to the bathroom, Sylvia went with me.

Archie tied my hands behind my back but left my feet untied. He made me lie down on the couch. I must have been exhausted because I dozed off. The sounds of two people making love woke me out of my sleep. My eyes followed the sound and watched Sylvia grind her hips on top of Archie. She must have felt me watching because she looked in my direction and smiled. She bent her upper body down and kissed him as they continued to have sex.

I wanted to puke for the umpteenth time in less than twenty-four hours. The sick part about all of it, she actually thought I was jealous. I was biding my time. I went back to sleep because I needed my energy. The clock in the room chimed three times waking me out

of my slumber. This time when I woke up, I heard
Archie and Sylvia snore. They were wrapped in each
other's arms without a care in the world.

My eyes adjusted to the darkness. I pushed myself
up. If I could make it to the bathroom and lock the
door, I could squeeze through the window. One thing
about a lot of the resort hotels, they didn't have glass
in the windows. It used to annoy me, but tonight I was
grateful.

The first few attempts I made to stand up were un-
successful. I fell back on the couch. I hoped the thump
wasn't enough to wake them up. The thump made me
realize that even if I made it to the bathroom, with the
ropes binding my hands behind my back, I wouldn't
be able to escape.

I whispered, "Sylvia." Each time, my voice would
escalate higher and higher until one of them stirred.

"Go see what she wants," Archie stated, before
turning back around.

Sylvia, with hair all over her head, walked over to
the couch. "What? I'm trying to get my beauty rest."

I wanted to say, "There's not enough sleep in the
world to cure you," but instead I said, "I need to use
the bathroom."

"Hurry up," she said, as she helped me up and
untied my arms. "I'm getting back in the bed. Don't
do anything stupid," she said.

Her stupidity worked in my favor. I ran the water, so
they couldn't hear me lock the door. I moved the chair
in the bathroom to the window. My first attempt almost
had me on the floor. I had better luck the second time,
but I wasn't quite quick enough. I heard Archie yell,
"Open the door." He attempted to turn the door knob.

He banged something against the door. I assumed it was his body.

I said a prayer and as I squeezed through the bathroom window, Archie attempted to grab my legs. I kicked and kicked until he released me. I fell to the ground. Once I realized my legs were okay, I took off running.

I began knocking on other patrons' doors. No one was answering. I could hear feet somewhere in the distance. I knew it was Archie and Sylvia but I was determined to find a safe haven. I saw a sign that said office and banged on the door. I yelled, "Help me! Somebody help me!"

A man who looked to be in his early twenties came to the door. "Ma'am are you okay?"

"Help me! Somebody's after me," I yelled. I felt like I was in a bad horror movie.

He let me in and shut the door and locked it.

"Call the police. I was kidnapped and they will kill you, me, and anybody else that gets in their way," I blurted.

He pushed me into another room and told me to lock the door. I did as I was told. I heard him call someone on the phone. The sound of a gun startled me. I could hear people screaming. I looked around to see if I could find a hiding place. I was trapped. There was nowhere else to hide. The handle on the door jiggled. I picked up a pair of scissors I saw on the desk and hid behind the door. If I was going to die, I was going out stabbing.

"Ma'am, they're gone. The police are on their way," the stranger stated.

He turned around to see me standing behind him

with the scissors. He reached his hands up and took them from my trembling hands. "Everything's okay."

The stranger held me in his arms to comfort me. I pulled back. "Did you get them?"

"I wounded one of them, but they got away," he said, sounding disappointed.

I extended my hand to make a formal introduction. "I'm Parris Mitchell."

He smiled. "I know. I recognized you once you said you were kidnapped."

"How?" I asked.

He pulled out his wallet and showed me his badge. "I'm Edward. By day, I'm an officer and by night onsite security."

For the first time in two days, I smiled. "Edward, I'm forever in your debt." I hugged him again.

"Watch out now. I'm a jealous man," Casper said.

Casper stood behind us with open arms. I ran into them and cried a river of tears. The warmth of his arms erased the pain of the last few hours. The police swarmed the place. After answering their questions, Edward escorted us to another hotel resort on Paradise Island.

I didn't exhale until we were safe and secure in a new room. Casper ran some bath water and insisted on helping me with my bath. My mind and body were too tired to argue. My body was sore all over and when I hit the hot water, I sighed. I leaned back and allowed the bubbles to cascade over my body. Casper lathered a washcloth with body wash. He took his time washing my neck, my back, and other body parts. His hand lingered between my legs and I closed my eyes and allowed him to bring me pleasure with the tips of his fingers. After oohing for several minutes, Casper continued to wash the rest of my body.

In spite of my ordeal, Casper had my body wanting him. As much as I protested, Casper insisted I needed rest. "Tonight you rest."

Cradled in his arms, I felt secure and went into a deep sleep. It was after four o'clock the next day when I awoke. At first it took me a minute to figure out my location. Casper was by my side before I could sit up. "I'm right here baby. I'm not leaving you ever again," he said.

"Casper, I'm fine."

He looked me in the eyes and said, "He didn't hurt . . . hurt you did he?"

I shook my head no. "Not in that way baby," I assured him.

I could hear him let out a breath of air. He held me tight and I could feel his rapid heartbeat. "I prayed that God would bring you back to me."

This time I was comforting him. "I'm right here. I'm not going anywhere."

We spent the evening holding each other and reassuring each other of our love for one another.

Carmen called several times, but I let Casper talk to her. "She's fine. She's just a little tired," I heard him say.

"Tell her I said thank you for keeping the media hounds at bay," I said.

He went back and forth delivering messages. "She heard you. She says she loves you and will meet us at the airport."

When he hung up, Casper said, "I don't know why you didn't talk to her yourself."

"Because I have you, silly," I said, as I threw a pillow at him.

We fought with the pillows for a few minutes before

ending up naked in between the sheets. "You complete me," Casper said, as he used his instrument of love to penetrate my physical and spiritual walls.

Although some of my muscles ached from the abduction, the pleasure Casper brought me overruled those senses. I wanted him to feel the same delight. Once on his back, I took to riding him as if he were a prize horse. Satisfied and waiting for the trophy at the end of the ride, no one person was in control, we rode to the finish line together.

He kissed my forehead before cradling me in his arms. "I love you," Casper said.

"I love you more," I responded.

Archie and Sylvia were on the loose but Casper wiped away my fears and insecurities; I felt completely satisfied. All I cared about at that moment was being with the man I loved.

"They got them," the pilot said over the intercom.

Casper walked to the cockpit to clarify. From the expression on Casper's face, I knew the pilot meant Archie and Sylvia. I wanted to jump up and down but remembered we were thousands of miles in the air. I survived being abducted, but I didn't think I could survive a plane crash. Everybody on the plane cheered. Casper popped the cork on a bottle of champagne and said, "Bubbly for everyone."

We celebrated their capture. We spent the rest of the plane ride laughing and talking. Casper catered to my every need. He held my hand throughout the majority of the plane ride.

* * *

All of the entertainment and news stations were waiting on us as soon as we exited the plane. Carmen met me at the gate and led me to a press area. Thanks to Carmen's quick thinking, I was prepared to answer most of the questions that came my way concerning Archie and Sylvia's capture. I was prepared to leave the podium when the annoying Sandy asked, "Since your album has wrapped, does that mean you and Casper are over?"

I spoke clearly into the microphone. "The question and answer session is over. Now if you'll excuse me, I've had enough excitement to last me a lifetime."

Cameras flashed, as Carmen, Casper, and the rest of our traveling party made it to our waiting limousines.

21

YOU DON'T HAVE
TO BE LONELY

I spent the next few weeks rehearsing and fighting
off the media. Archie and Sylvia's capture was the talk
of the town. Casper leaked the new single "You Don't
Have To Be Lonely" on the Internet by having his assistant post it to message boards and various Web
sites. Carmen used the opportunity to promote my CD.

"Girl, you need to send Archie a care package filled
with hot coals, because your CD will be flying off the
shelves after I finish working this media attention."
Carmen joked.

The interview I did with Black Essence television
squashed all the rumors and confirmed Casper and I
were still an item. The tabloids had a field day with the
Bahamas story and swore Casper found Archie and
beat him black and blue. We laughed because Casper
imagined doing just that. They also had me pulling off

Sylvia's wig. According to their sources, I slapped off her fake nails too. Goes to show you that you can't believe everything you read.

After begging my mom, I finally convinced her to fly to Los Angeles for the BEAM awards. Although, I wasn't up for an award, this was one of the biggest performances of my career. I had something to prove and I was determined to do it on this scheduled night.

Casper informed me that Xavier was flying in too. I had heard the same from Carmen. Carmen won't admit it, but her relationship with Xavier is more serious than she says. I don't know why the secrecy. Besides, if Casper and I can get past our five-year age difference, Xavier being two years younger than she, shouldn't be an issue.

"Mama, I'm so glad to see you." I ran up to her and hugged her when she exited the plane.

"Child, remind me not to drink so much on my return flight. My bladder had me running to the bathroom all through the flight." She talked nonstop.

It was good seeing her. We had only spent a few days together. I chastised myself for not visiting my mom more often. Casper was waiting for us at my place. He greeted us at the door.

"So this is the young man who has my daughter's heart." She hugged him as if they had met before.

"Yes, ma'am. She has mine too," he said, before picking up her bags and taking them to the downstairs guest bedroom.

"Let's talk." Mom followed Casper.

"Mom. You just met him."

She ignored me.

I threw my hands up in the air as I watched my mom follow Casper to interrogate him. I don't know what I was worried about. My mom and Casper hit it off. In fact, he kept her entertained while I rehearsed. The awards show was coming up and our last rehearsal would be at the Staples Center.

"Carmen, this is it," I said, as the rehearsal ended.

"You picked the right song."

"Wait until you hear the remix."

"Girl, I'm late." Carmen glanced at her watch and swooped up her handbag. "Catch you later." She hugged me before rushing out.

"Xavier will wait," I yelled.

She threw her hand up in the air to acknowledge she heard me but kept walking.

My mom cooked us a good southern breakfast filled with homemade biscuits, bacon, scrambled eggs, sausage, grits, and hash browns. By the time she was finished cooking, it was closer to noon, so I guess I should have said it was brunch.

Xavier and Carmen walked in with Casper. Casper hugged my mom and kissed her on the cheek before I got my kiss. I pretended to be offended.

"No, you can keep your kisses now. Giving my sugar to another woman." I playfully pushed him away.

"Now baby, you know I only have sugar for you." He placed kisses on my face and eventually on my lips.

Xavier cleared his throat. "Stop before you spoil my appetite."

Carmen hit him on the arm. "Don't be jealous."

My mom didn't bite her tongue. "You two might as well let the cat out of the bag."

Carmen pretended to ignore her, but that's one thing you don't do. "I don't know what you're talking about."

"Love is in the air," my mom hummed. I got my beautiful voice from her.

Carmen almost choked on the gum she was chewing. "We're just friends."

"Uh-huh," was all my mom would say. "Anyway, eat up before your food gets cold."

After breakfast, I left everyone downstairs to get a few minutes alone. I didn't realize my mom was following me. When I walked out on my balcony, she was behind me.

"You okay?" she asked.

"Just a little nervous about tonight." I hadn't admitted this to anyone, not even Casper.

She wrapped her arms around my shoulders. "You'll do fine. Look for me in the audience like you used to do when you first started. Remember?"

I looked at her and smiled. "Yes. As long as I could see your face, I knew everything was going to be all right."

We walked back in arm in arm. "So if you find yourself getting nervous, I'll be sitting right there on the front row." She paused. "I will be on the front row won't I?"

I laughed. "Yes, Mom. We have some of the best seats in the house."

Casper was entering my room as we walked back in. "I was wondering where my two favorite girls went."

"Two? Mom, I knew you were after my man." I joked.

"With looks like these he couldn't resist." She patted her hair and twisted away.

Casper and I couldn't stop laughing.

"Casper's here," my mother yelled up from downstairs.

I looked in the mirror. The long pink custom-made dress fell over the curves of my body. The long split up the side accented the diamond-studded stockings I wore. I slipped on the diamond-studded pink-laced pumps to match. I looked at my hand one last time and admired the engagement ring I was wearing before finding my matching pink satin purse.

When I made it down the stairs, my mom was beautifully dressed in the custom-made black dress I had a designer make for her. She looked exquisite.

Casper was wearing a black pinstriped tuxedo. I wanted to run into his arms, but resisted. "You look great as usual," he commented.

"So do you." I couldn't resist planting a kiss on his tantalizing lips.

My mom cleared her throat. I wiped the lipstick from Casper's lips.

"Ladies, are you ready?" he asked, as he opened the door.

He locked up and we followed him down the walkway to the waiting long black stretch limousine.

Cameras flashed out of control when we made it to the Staples Center and walked the red carpet. I did preshow interviews with all the major stations. Sandy did her best to get an interview, but I shunned her.

"Isn't that Sandy Blair?" my mom asked, as I hurried her along.

I made sure my mom was in eyesight as reporters asked Casper and me questions. To my relief, we made it inside without incident. Xavier and Carmen met us inside. Their seats were right behind ours. I don't know how Carmen managed that, but knowing her, she called in some favors. I looked up when I heard someone call my name. Lance, dressed in a black tuxedo, and Rose, wearing one of her designs, sashayed over. Casper and I stood up to greet them. Rose sat in the seat next to mine.

"We've set a date," Rose said.

"It's about time," Casper jokingly said.

I gave him a "don't go there look" and turned back around to face Rose. "I have the perfect song too."

We chatted about their wedding and spoke to different people we knew. My mom knew some of Rose's relatives back in Shreveport so she updated Rose on hometown gossip. I wasn't one of the first performers, so we had to sit through a quarter of the show before it was time for me to present the Best New R & B Female Singer award. After a commercial break, I was to perform.

"Baby, you're going to do fine." Casper got up and kissed me on the cheek before I walked away.

I left him and my mom sitting in the front row.

Sierra, the winner of the Best New R & B Female Award I handed out, was so excited that she forgot to take the statue I was holding for her. I had to run behind her to catch up with her. "You just don't know what this night means to me. To get this award—and from my idol," Sierra said.

I hugged her as cameras flashed backstage. "You

deserve it dear. Now go." I rushed her along to enjoy being in the spotlight.

I made my way to my designated dressing room to change. The butterflies in my stomach wouldn't stop until after my performance. The outfit I was now wearing made me look ten years younger and if you didn't know I was thirty-two, you would have sworn I was in my early twenties. I wore the black miniskirt as if it were a second skin. Working out had paid off. I could put Janet's abs to shame now.

When it was announced I was about to enter the stage, I could hear the applause. The adrenaline built up and after making sure everybody was ready and in place, I flipped the microphone on and walked out onstage. I was nervous, but was soon over it as I felt the love from people in the room. Nobody knew what to expect, so this was my opportunity to shine.

The dancers were doing their thing as I danced my way to the front. The beat was electrifying. From the time I opened my mouth and sang the first lyrics, "You don't have to be lonely . . . only if you want to be" the audience was under my spell. The stage was mine and I milked it for all it was worth.

At the end of my performance, I got a standing ovation. I looked at Casper and my mom in the crowd and blew them a kiss. The reporters were waiting for me backstage with hundreds of questions. All I could hear was my named being called in all directions. Carmen came out and rescued me. We went to the podium and answered a few questions.

"It'll be my first single and will be available this Tuesday across the country."

Carmen was thrilled I didn't forget to mention it. I'm sure the record company was too.

* * *

After the awards show, Casper and I decided not to attend any of the parties. Carmen and Xavier vowed to hit as many as they could. I needed to get Casper alone and although he hadn't pressured me for an answer for his proposal, I knew he was getting antsy about it. The limousine dropped us off at home.

"I'm so proud of you, baby," Mama said before kissing me on the cheek and retiring for the night.

Casper was unusually quiet.

"Come, there's something we need to talk about." I grabbed his hand and we walked outside onto the patio.

The sky was cloudy, but it was still a beautiful night. Casper sat in one of the patio chairs and pulled me onto this lap. I loosened his tie. I placed my arms around his neck and gazed into his eyes. I decided not to keep him in suspense any longer. "The answer is *yes*."

He didn't say anything so I was concerned. Questions went through my mind. Has he changed his mind about marrying me? Nervousness set in.

After a few seconds, his voice crackled when he asked, "Yes to what?"

I stated, "Casper, I will be honored to be your wife."

"Baby, you've made me the happiest man alive."

We kissed. He ran his hand through my hair releasing the curls that were pinned up.

"I love you," I said as I laid my head on his shoulder.

"I love you too."

"Thank you." I added.

"For what?" he asked as he stroked my back.

I looked into his loving eyes, "For bringing out the best in me."

22

PLEASE DON'T GO

Casper and I agreed to a long engagement. I wanted to make sure we were ready. He proved to me time and time again that he would always put my best interest first. We set the date for a year after my BEAM award comeback performance.

The headlines all across the country read "She's Back." The performance at the BEAMs strengthened my return to the music scene. The record company was happy. I was now in a position to decide on where I wanted to be. I hadn't decided on whether to stay with them or go with a new company.

I logged onto my computer as "songbird" and read the message boards. The fans loved my performance and my single was number one on the R & B and pop charts. It was hard not getting caught up in the whirlwind of being back on top. With a support system like my mom, Casper, Mason, and Carmen, they made sure I stayed grounded.

The duet with Rose got released to promote her upcoming movie. Casper handed me the latest *Billboard* results before taking a seat next to me. "How do you feel about your duet battling with your single for the number one spot?"

"You got to be kidding," I said, as I scanned and saw both songs battling it out. I was elated.

Casper watched me do my happy dance, which in turn excited him to join me. "I hope you're this happy on our wedding day," Casper said as he twirled me around.

I leaned my head back and basked in the joy of being in his arms. "On our wedding night we're going to dance the night away."

He pulled me closer to him and kissed me. "Dancing will be the last thing on your mind on our wedding night."

Our dance led to a tango between the sheets. He dipped and I did a crescendo. The final encore found us entwined until the next morning.

"Rose's wedding is in a few days and I still don't know what I'm wearing," I said, from my closet. "Hand me the phone," I said.

Casper stood in the doorway with my cell phone in his hands. I looked at him and said, "Are you going to walk it over here?"

He didn't move. "I'm not your butler."

I walked to the doorway and snatched the phone from his hands. "But you would make a cute one if you were." I didn't wait for him to respond. I dialed Fazio, one of my favorite new designers, to see if he had a dress for the occasion.

"Why did you wait to the last minute?" Fazio asked.

I listened to him lecture me about being more prepared for events like this. "I owe you," I said.

"If you let me design your wedding dress, we can
call it even," he responded.

I hadn't thought that far ahead, but I said, "Sure."

Fazio went on and on about Rose's wedding. I had
other things to do, but I knew better than to rush him
or else I would be back to looking for a dress to wear.
Fifteen minutes later, our conversation ended.

Casper was nowhere to be found. "He could have
told me he was leaving," I pouted.

"She doesn't need to know," I heard Casper tell
someone.

I walked through the patio door and opened my
mouth to speak when I saw Casper's hand go up indi-
cating for me to wait. I folded my arms. Archie was
the last man I gave control too and if Casper thought
he could control what I did or didn't do he was in for
a rude awakening. The moment I knew he was off the
call, I said, "Don't be making decisions without con-
sulting me."

Casper looked at me as if I had two heads. "The
next time you eavesdrop, make sure you hear the
whole story."

Last night we couldn't keep our hands off each other,
but today we were about to bite the heads off each other.
Maybe we had been spending too much time together.
I don't know, but whatever it was, I hoped we dealt with
it soon because I don't like tension. "Casper we need to
talk," I said, leaving him looking at my backside. I
waited for him to follow me, but he didn't. I walked
back out the patio door and he remained in his same
seat. I said, "Why didn't you follow me?"

His response caught me off guard. "You've been in full diva mode and frankly I'm tired of it."

I batted my eyes. I opened my mouth to say something, but couldn't think of a smart response. "I'm tired of everybody trying to run my life."

Casper stood up. "Is that really how you feel?"

I stuck my lips out. "I wouldn't have said it if I didn't mean it."

The look on Casper's face let me know I'd taken things too far. He moved past me and toward the patio door. "I'm leaving before I say something we both regret."

That should have been my cue to drop it, but instead I walked behind him and yelled, "Don't be afraid. Speak your mind. Don't be a punk."

He turned around and grabbed me by the arm. "I'm nobody's punk and the next time you walk behind me like that, it better be to hug me." He dropped my arm. "I'm out."

I stood in the same spot because I was shocked he grabbed me. I would show him. He could take his punk behind home for all I cared. I looked at the ring and was about to take it off and throw it at him, but when I got ready to pull it off, my heart tugged and I couldn't. I wanted to say, "Please, don't go."

When I heard the door slam, I shouted, "Run. I'm used to men running away." I leaned against the door and my body slid down. I cradled my face with my hands as tears flowed nonstop. I'd overreacted but didn't feel like apologizing. Pride could damage a relationship.

I thought Casper and I would kiss and make up, but after a few days of playing phone tag, I was beginning to think more was going on than I figured. He refused to answer any of my calls and I let his calls go to voice mail when he returned my calls. Mason thought I should be the one to apologize since I did go off for no reason. I disagreed, but knew in my heart, she was right. After the fourth day of not talking to Casper, I threw on a jogging suit and drove over to his place.

I used my key and disarmed the alarm. I could have called, but I wanted to surprise him. Instead I was in for a surprise when I saw a half-naked woman run from the guest bedroom to the guest bathroom. I took off my earrings. I took off my high-heel shoes. I cracked my knuckles because it was about to be a throwdown. Both doors were closed. I waited outside for the woman to exit the bathroom. She would be in for a surprise. When I heard the bathroom door open, with a tight fist, I pulled my arm back and was ready to coldcock her in the face. The moment I reared back to hit her, I felt a tug on my arm.

"Parris, what are you doing?" Casper asked.

I wiggled from his arm. The woman wailed. Peter opened the door wearing a pair of silk boxers. The woman slammed the door shut. "Baby, you can come out," Peter said.

"Baby?" I said, as I looked between Casper and Peter.

"You didn't think she and I were . . ." Casper didn't finish his statement. He looked disappointed because I didn't deny what he said. "Peter, man I'm sorry. Come on Parris," Casper said, as he took my hand and led me to another part of the house.

I felt like a fool. How was I supposed to know she was Peter's woman? In fact, why was Peter at Casper's? "I'm sorry. Is that what you want to hear?" I blurted out as we sat across from each other on the sofa in his den.

"You can save that sorry apology."

I didn't like his tone. For someone who should have been happy to see me, he seemed infuriated. Something was going on and I needed to find out now. Mama always said you could catch more bees with honey, so I poured it on thick. I stood up and walked behind him. I knew he couldn't resist my shoulder massage. At first he acted as if he wanted to move away from my hands, but after a few minutes, he allowed me to work the tension out of his shoulders. It took extra strength to loosen up his muscles. I heard him moan. I knew it was time to make my move. I leaned down and kissed him on his neck.

Before I realized it, Casper had pulled me across the sofa and we were lip-locking. "I accept your apology," Casper stated.

"I admit. I've been a little full of myself lately," I said. Casper cleared his throat. I continued to say, "Okay, a lot."

"It's hard to stay mad at you," Casper said. By now, I'm sitting in his lap.

"You could have fooled me. It's been four days." I held my hand up and used my fingers to count down. He kissed each one.

"You forgot I had a meeting in New York. I just got back today," Casper stated. Actually, I was so caught up in my own schedule I had forgotten about his planned trip.

"My bad," I said. Casper kissed my neck. I moaned, "Stop it before Peter and his woman walk in on something."

Peter and his woman stood fully dressed. "Parris, this is Belinda. Belinda, this is Parris."

I don't blame Belinda for not giving me a warmer greeting. I removed myself from Casper's lap and stood up to shake her hand. "Sorry for the misunderstanding. See, I thought you and Casper . . ." It didn't sound good so I stopped.

"If someone was in Peter's house I would have done the same thing," Belinda interrupted.

I felt relieved. Peter caught me up on things with him. One of his pipes broke and flooded his apartment. His new house wouldn't be ready until next week, so he was staying with Casper in the interim.

"The girlfriend is always the last one to know," I said.

"Girlfriend?" Casper asked while looking at my engagement ring.

I held my hand up to show off my ring. "Excuse me. I mean fiancée."

Belinda and I decided to cook our men dinner. While preparing the meal, Belinda shared with me how she met Peter and how she was hoping their moving into a house would be the push he needed to pop the question to her. "If he doesn't, you need to start rationing out the goodies," I said, while sampling my spaghetti sauce.

"I tried that before and the only thing I ended up doing was throwing away stained towels."

I scrunched up my face and said, "Ugghh."

"Imagine how I felt when I saw them in the towel hamper."

I held out my hand in protest. "Enough. No more please."

Peter and Casper walked into the kitchen. "What's up ladies?" Casper asked as he took a few cans of soda from the refrigerator.

"Nothing I want to repeat." I looked at Belinda and we burst out laughing.

23

YOUR LOVE
IS ALL I NEED

"That's a wrap," Danny, the best choreographer I knew, said, as he pushed me and my dance team to the next level.

I stopped, wiped the sweat from my forehead and bent over. Danny was wearing me out. "I don't know if I can do this. This body ain't as young as it used to be."

Danny was by my side before I could stand back up. "You can and you will. Now hop back to it."

We rehearsed for a few more hours. My tour was scheduled to launch in Los Angeles and would end in Paris, France. Most of my previous background dancers were set to go with me. "Ladies and gents, I'll see you Sunday morning," I said.

The dancers scattered and went to their separate destinations. I was gathering up my things when Danny walked up and said, "I heard you were singing at Rose's wedding."

"Yes. I'm going to be busy. Rose's wedding's on Saturday and the concert on Sunday."

We talked about weddings as we walked to the parking garage together. I gave him a hug. I watched him walk to his car and shook my head. "What a waste of a good man. He would have made a good boyfriend." I backed up and honked my horn as I drove by Danny getting in his pink Corvette.

"But baby," I moaned.

Casper held my hand as he talked. "This is how I make my money."

My other hand held the concert schedule. I threw it toward the table. It landed on the floor. "I thought you would at least be able to make some of the weekend concerts."

Casper removed his hand from mine and picked up the paper before scanning it and placing it on the table. "Let's just play it by ear."

I couldn't mask my disappointment. The selfish side of me wanted him at every concert, but I had resigned myself to think he would at least be at my weekend shows. Now I had to listen to him tell me he didn't know about those. I would be on the road for the next three or four months and that was a long time to be away from the man I loved.

My body responded to Casper's touches. Every time we disagreed about something, he knew exactly what to do to get my mind off the issue. This time I refused to let it work. This time. "Ooh," I moaned.

I jumped up. "I need to take a shower."

Casper stood beside me. "I'll join you."

There goes my plan to get away. We held hands as we walked up the stairs to my bathroom. Two hours later, we were spread out across the bed in need of another shower after his five-star performances between the sheets. We were both too exhausted to move.

He snored and smiled in his sleep. I kissed his forehead and went to sleep.

I hit the snooze button on the alarm several times. After noticing the clock read 9:00, I slid from beneath the covers. Casper asked, "Where are you going?"

"Spa day. Rose is treating all of the wedding party to a day at the spa and I'm late."

He rubbed his eyes and looked at the clock. "It's only nine o'clock."

"And the limo will be here to pick me up at nine-thirty," I said, while leaving Casper in the bed.

It was nine forty-five by the time I made it outside. I apologized to the driver. Rose, Carmen, Rose's twin sister Violet, and a few people I didn't know were waiting for me in the limousine.

Once inside I said, "Sorry, I'm late. Casper had me up late and I overslept." I knew it wasn't Casper's fault, but I had to blame it on somebody and he wasn't here.

Rose said, "As fine as he is, I don't blame you for being late."

"You're getting married, so you shouldn't be worried about someone else's man," a lady with a southern accent said.

Rose rolled her eyes at her. She poured me a glass of champagne and handed it to me. "This is to my last day of freedom and to a lifetime of uninhibited sex."

We looked from one to another. Rose continued to say, "Just kidding. I'm already having that."

Our glasses clinked as we laughed, talked, and drank. By the time we made it to the spa, we were more than relaxed; we were tipsy. The next four hours were spent getting massages, facials, manicures and pedicures. I was excited after returning from a day of pampering.

Casper's scent lingered in the air. To my disappointment, he was nowhere to be found. I dialed his cell phone. "Where are you?" I asked.

"I'll meet you tonight. I needed to take care of a few things before tomorrow," he replied.

"Don't be too long. I have something for you," I purred.

After hanging up with him, I called my mom and then Mason. I spent the next few hours on the phone. Casper couldn't make it to the wedding rehearsal with me, but met me for the rehearsal dinner. We had a good time socializing with Rose and her family. I was surprised to learn that her sister Violet was also engaged to be married. I didn't know Violet personally but I was proud that another woman from my hometown had made it. We Louisiana girls had to stick together.

"The next time I see you, you'll be ready to walk down the aisle," I said to Rose before leaving.

"Thanks again for agreeing to sing at the wedding," Rose said, as she hugged me and Casper good-bye.

Cameras flashed. I sighed.

"It's going to be worse tomorrow," Rose commented.

I waved at everybody and followed Casper to his car.

I refused to watch television before Rose's wedding. I hoped Rose hadn't read the morning paper because my favorite reporter Sandy reported Lance got buck wild at his bachelor party. I asked Casper about it and he denied knowing anything about it. He's a man so I didn't expect him to reveal anything. "You better not have any strippers at yours is all I can say," I said.

"I don't know why you read that mess. You know as well as I know, most of that stuff is bull," he responded.

When I looked up, he was smiling and his eyes twinkled. I said, "Fine. Don't tell me what happened at the party. I don't want to know anyway." I threw the paper down and headed upstairs.

I had an ensemble of people help me get ready. One of the designer's assistants helped me with my dress. My hairdresser did my hair and a makeup artist put the finishing touches of my makeup. Although they were not invited to the wedding, they were as excited about it as I was.

Casper knocked on the door to let me know it was time. "I'll meet you downstairs," I yelled.

After making sure everybody was out of my room. I did a quick glance in the mirror. Casper stood at the end of the stairway with his mouth hanging open. He watched me glide down the stairs in my pink ankle-length silk beaded chiffon dress. The dress accented every curve of my body. The working out and eating right paid off, because the dress fit perfectly.

Casper said, "Baby, you're going to outshine the bride. And you know Rose ain't having that."

I giggled. "I do look good, don't I?"

The limousine drive over to the church took longer than expected. We had to dodge reporters and cameras so the driver was instructed to take the long route. We only had twenty minutes to spare before the wedding was supposed to start.

Pink and white roses adorned the pews. The church was filled to capacity. After signing the guestbook, we were escorted to our seats. "Everything is so beautiful," I said to Casper, as we sat down.

There were many of our celebrity friends present, so conversations were aplenty. My stomach felt funny. I whispered to Casper, "I'm getting butterflies."

He stroked my hand for assurance. "You'll do fine baby." He kissed me on the cheek right before I stood up to go wait in my position.

I got a good view of the entire church as I stood and watched the wedding coordinator whisper something in the pianist's ear. The music changed and the rest of the church got quiet. The preacher, Lance, and his best man walked in to stand at the front of the church.

The five bridesmaids walked down the aisle with the groomsmen. Violet looked beautiful as she floated down the aisle wearing a different shade of pink from the bridesmaids. Her dress was also shorter.

It was now my time to shine. I stood behind the microphone and waited for my keyboardist to exchange seats with the pianist. We got our cue from the wedding coordinator. The music started and I sang, "I never thought I would find someone like you . . . I never thought I could be as happy as the way you make me feel . . . I never knew a love like this before . . . your love is all I need . . ."

Everyone stood up. As I continued to sing, Rose, wearing an off-white beaded straight-laced gown and tiara, walked down the aisle escorted by her uncle. She made a beautiful bride. Once I was through singing my song, I went and sat by Casper. He kissed me on the lips. I smiled. We held hands throughout the entire ceremony. I don't know what he was thinking but I was thinking about our wedding day. I couldn't wait to be his wife.

The media had a field day. Reporters were sticking microphones in our faces as we tried to leave the church. Casper blocked them as best as he could. One reporter said, "Will the song you sang today be on your next CD?"

I smiled and said, "No. It was written especially for today."

Sandy said, "When is your wedding?"

Casper said, "Soon. Now excuse us." Casper placed his arm around me as we continued to walk to our limousine.

We didn't spend a long time at the reception because we were too anxious to have our own private celebration. It wasn't our wedding but we partied as if it were. Later that night, Casper and I had a prehoney-moon rehearsal.

24

DROP IT

The two opening acts did a great job warming up the crowd. I watched the monitor stationed backstage. The crowd was loud and bodacious; just the way I liked them when I performed. With an accelerated heartbeat, I had to breathe in and out to calm my nerves. Casper waited for me back in my dressing room. The room was filled with flowers from other celebrities.

Casper shook his head. "If you didn't have to perform, I would tear that outfit off you right now."

Here I was set to go perform in front of thousands and Casper had me blushing. He walked with me to meet my crew. We huddled around each other and I said a prayer. "Let's do this," I said, as we went to the stage.

"Are y'all ready to party?" I asked.

The crowd screamed, "Yes."

"Band, give them what they want," I yelled. We performed one of my first hits. It was magical watching the audience sing along with me.

I changed outfits a few times. For this next session, I wanted something slinky, but sexy. It was time to slow the tempo down. I asked the crowd, "Have you ever been in love?"

Some yelled, "Yeah."

I started off talking, "I don't know about y'all, but sometimes love will make you do some crazy things. Sometimes love will make you put up with some crazy things." I went on to sing the lyrics to another hit song from the past.

In my last set, I sang my newer songs. "You don't have to be lonely . . . only if you want to be . . ." The crowd swayed along with me as I rocked the stage.

I performed for two hours and although exhausting, it was fulfilling. I went back onstage for a few encores. I missed this. I missed performing. I missed the sound of adoring fans screaming my name. I missed the spotlight. All eyes being on me is what I missed.

It took me a little while to come down off that performance high. Casper rubbed my feet on the ride from the concert hall to the after-party. "Baby, there's no one else like you," he said, as he bent down and kissed my foot.

I leaned back and enjoyed it. I moved my foot. "If you start that, I'll be telling the driver to take us home."

We laughed. When we got to the club, the front entranceway was crowded. Casper made a quick phone call. "Take us around back," he said to the limousine driver.

Once inside the club, we headed to the VIP area. It was filled with celebrities from music, movies, and sports. Everyone took the time to congratulate me on a show well done. I had made a conscious effort not to be what Casper called "in my diva mode" around him, but since this was my night, Casper moved to the side and allowed me my moment in the spotlight.

People were taking pictures left and right. I was still in a party mood, so between dancing with Casper and other people I knew, the paparazzi cameras flashing didn't dampen my mood. In fact, seeing Sandy there only made me party a little harder.

"Drop it, don't break it," Casper shouted as he danced behind me.

We didn't make it home until after four the next morning.

The next day when I woke up, I heard Casper moving around the bedroom. I pulled the covers tighter, covering my head. "Wake me up tomorrow," I said.

"No can do. You told me not to let you sleep the day away," he responded.

I slowly pulled the covers down as my eyes adjusted to the beaming sunlight creeping through the curtains. Reluctantly I sat up. Casper held the newspaper under his arm as he placed a tray of fresh fruit and juice in front of me. "Aren't you going to eat something?" I asked.

"Already did. Now eat up. Turn to page E-1," he said, as he left the room. A few minutes later I heard the water from the shower running.

I glanced at the front page of the newspaper. A small caption and picture of me performing from the previous night were displayed in the upper right hand corner. I discarded the rest of the newspaper and pulled out the entertainment section.

There were several pictures from last night's performance. The pictures showed me in several different outfits. The review was glowing. Of course Sandy had something negative to say about me on page two about my after-party, but her words were not enough to spoil the fact the *Times* gave my performance five stars.

I slipped into the shower behind Casper. I massaged him. He moaned. I wouldn't allow him to turn around. I made sure he got pleasured before letting him pleasure me. My hair was soaked but my body was satisfied after our shower interlude.

"I'm going to miss you," Casper said, as he put on his socks.

With a towel still wrapped around me, I jumped on the bed and attempted to pull him down to me. "I'm going to miss you more."

We kissed but I wouldn't allow it to go further, because I didn't want to be the reason why Casper was late for his flight. I threw on my robe and walked him to the door. "I'll see you in Dallas at the end of the week," I said, right before Casper leaned down and kissed me.

"Keep your phone charged," Casper said. He kissed me on my forehead and went out the door.

A long tear fell down my right cheek. I had to pull myself together. "A man doesn't define me," I chanted.

I gave my housekeeper strict instructions on what to do in my absence. Carmen agreed to do spot checks to make sure she wasn't having house parties in my absence. I had one stop to make before my flight left. I didn't want to do it, but Carmen insisted it would help boost ticket sales.

The producer of the talk show led me to a dressing room. "If you need anything else, let me know," he said, while holding a clipboard in one hand and his phone in the other.

I was swarmed with hair and makeup artists. I watched the monitor in the room. The announcer said to the audience, "Welcome to the *Hailey Barnes Show*."

I waited backstage while I watched Hailey do her opening commentary. When the music played, the associate producer prompted me to enter the stage. Hailey stood and we hugged.

"Can you believe it, I'm here with Parris Mitchell," Hailey said, sounding excited.

My palms sweated. Hailey was famous for catching her guests off guard with some hard and personal questions. I mentally cursed Carmen out for setting this up. Hailey showed footage from the time I was twenty-one until more recently. "So tell me. How does it feel being back on top?" Hailey asked.

"I was born to do this," I responded. "Life can be a roller-coaster ride, but you can't allow it to keep you down."

"Exactly. We'll be right back after this commercial," Hailey looked into the camera and said.

A crew member brought us over two bottled waters. I took a sip out of mine. For some reason my throat felt extra dry.

Hailey assured me. "You're doing fine. I need to warn you the next set will be more intense."

Before I could ask her what she meant by it, the cameras were back rolling. Hailey said, "As you know Parris is a media magnet. We can't get enough of her."

I smiled and waited for her next question. She got comfortable in her chair. "How do you deal with meddlesome reporters? Excluding myself of course." She giggled.

I took a deep breath before responding. "We all have a job to do. Reporters are only doing their jobs;

however, they must understand that although we may be celebrities we are entitled to a private life."

"Some of the public might disagree," Hailey responded.

I elaborated. "I love my fans and I don't have a problem with most reporters. If I'm eating, at least give me those minutes of peace. Like most women across the country, shopping is fun, but when I get bombarded by the paparazzi, it takes the joy away."

Hailey's facial expression changed to empathy. "I can relate to that," she said. She added, "Since we're on this subject, let's squash some rumors now. Some reporter, who will go nameless, she knows who she is, claimed there was some animosity between me and Parris."

I looked directly into the cameras. "If there were, would I be on your show? I think not."

The producer played some music that he usually plays when Hailey claims to squash a rumor.

We spent the rest of the interview talking about fashion and my new CD.

One of the last questions she asked concerned Casper. "Your fans and I want to know, when is the big day?"

She grabbed my hand and held it up as the camera zoomed on my engagement ring. I blushed. "Hailey, we're still making plans, but you'll be one of the first to know."

"I'll hold you to it."

She did her closing commentary. We both greeted audience members. I posed for pictures and signed autographs. I followed Hailey to the back of the stage about an hour later.

"Thanks for coming on the show. The audience loved you," Hailey stated.

I had to increase my pace to keep up with her as she walked. "No problem." Now that we weren't in front of the cameras, I didn't want a confrontation. Hailey and I weren't enemies, but we weren't friends either.

"Tell Casper I said hello."

"Will do," I responded.

"Maybe I can have you both on the show when you decide on your wedding date," she said.

"We'll see," I responded.

She hugged me as if we were best buddies and said, "Good luck on the rest of your tour."

She didn't wait for me to respond. She left me standing in the hallway. I grabbed my personal items and left to catch my flight.

25

MY BOO

Casper and I talked in between his meetings and my rehearsals and concerts. Although he met me in Dallas, it was two weeks afterward before we met up again. He was working with a client in New York and promised to meet me at my hotel.

"Girl, I've missed you," Casper said, as he wrapped his arms around me after our quick love session.

I kissed his arm. "I needed that."

"I love you," Casper said.

"I love you too," I responded.

He stirred beside me. "We need to talk," he said.

"Can it wait?" I wanted to savor this time in his arms.

"Yeah, I guess," he said.

Now I was curious to what weighed so heavily on his mind. I attempted to go to sleep, but didn't sleep well. When my alarm went off at five, my head felt like a brick had hit it.

I was scheduled to be on a few morning shows so I couldn't afford to be late. I washed my face and noticed the bags under my eyes. I called my makeup artist to my room. After getting dressed and meeting my crew downstairs, I said my good-byes to Casper and went on my talk show tour. Casper never told me what he had to say from last night.

The *Morning Show* had me performing to an enthusiastic crowd. The record company donated some CDs so I threw a few out into the crowd. My final talk show stop was with Regis. The audience loved my new single. Kelly danced along with my background dancers.

Casper met up with me later that night at the Madison Square Garden concert. His presence calmed me. We had a nightly ritual. He would call me every night right before I went onstage. After the opening acts performed, I took to the stage. The crowd sang along to my old and new hits. I had the whole place rocking and holding up their flashlights when the engineer turned the lights out.

The performance in New York hit the entertainment headlines across the country the next day. My next stop was Toronto and after performing in Canada on a few stops, I was headed to Europe. Casper had some downtime so he accompanied me on the Canadian tour. When it was time for me to leave for Europe, I became depressed.

"You knew I couldn't go, so stop pouting," Casper said, as he cradled me in his arms.

"A month is a long time," I complained.

"Time will go by so fast. We have our phones, laptops. We'll be communicating," he assured me.

* * *

I traveled to over seven countries and sang to sold-out stadiums. The European elite welcomed me with open arms. Carmen kept me abreast of what was going on in the States. Although Sandy wasn't here to pour out her venom in print, she made sure she kept drama going back in the States.

Maybe one day I would find out why she seemed to have a personal vendetta to persecute me in the press every chance she got. For now, I enjoyed the fact that the media in Europe wrote nothing but good things about me. My tour was coming to an end. My friends were scheduled to meet me in Paris for the tour finale.

I treated my crew to a day of pampering. Some of the men protested but after convincing them that they would be catered to by beautiful women, they quickly changed their minds.

"Ms. Mitchell, there's a gentleman downstairs who says you're expecting him. A Casper Johnson," the hotel clerk said at the other end of the phone.

"Yes, he's my fiancé. Let him up."

Security was tight. Although I gave them a list of my visitors, they were told to not let anyone up to my floor who didn't have a key. I made a mental note to tell them that checking IDs and matching them to their list would suffice.

I ran my hands through my curly bouncy auburn hair. I greeted Casper at the door. Our lips locked and we could barely keep our hands off each other. We agreed to not let this much time keep us away from each other ever again.

We were lounging in bed when Mason called to inform me she and my mom were checking in to the hotel. She gave me their room numbers. I jumped up. Casper turned over to his other side. I shook him. "Wake up. Mason's here. My mom's here."

"No. Wake me up later," he said, without opening his eyes.

I jumped back on the bed and straddled him while he lay on his side. I began to tickle him.

He complained. "You don't play fair."

"I know." I got up and threw the pillow at him before walking away from the bed.

An hour later, Casper and I met up with Mason and my mom. He treated us to lunch in the hotel restaurant. Casper left to go hang out with some of the guys in the band so we could have some alone time.

"He keeps getting finer and finer," Mason said, once Casper was out of the room.

I agreed. We were chatting and walking to the elevator when I noticed Casper talking to Rose and Lance. "I'll meet y'all upstairs," I said, before walking away.

"Did you know they were coming?" I asked Casper, as I hugged Rose and Lance.

"This was a surprise to me too," he responded.

Rose said, "We couldn't make your first show due to . . ." Rose glanced at Lance. They smiled at each other. She continued to say, "Our wedding, but we definitely wanted to be here to support you as you ended what I hear was a fantastic tour."

We chatted about their wedding and Lance Jr. as we rode up the elevator. We were all staying on the same floor. After saying our good-byes, Casper and I went to our room to get ready for the dinner party that was planned.

Carmen and Xavier made a grand entrance. For two people who were only friends, they spent a lot of time together. Xavier's hand on the small of Carmen's back spoke volumes. He gave men a strange look when it seemed like they were getting too close to Carmen. Carmen was doing what she loved to do, socializing. I introduced her to several dukes and duchesses.

I attempted to keep an eye out on all of my special guests, but it was becoming stressful. Casper must have sensed it because he whisked me away to an outside balcony. The stars shined bright as the half moon appeared to be dangling from the sky. We slow danced to the ballroom music. He dipped me and said, "It's my duty to take care of you, since you're so busy taking care of everybody else," he said.

"You won't get any complaints here," I responded.

Mason yelled from the doorway, "They are looking for you."

"Duty calls," I said, as I led Casper back inside.

After a speech by the Duke of Wingenburg, I spoke and thanked everyone for being there. I spent the rest of the night talking and dancing. By the time, Casper and I returned to our room, we were too exhausted to do anything but sleep.

"Thank you all for everything. I couldn't have done this without any of you," I said, as I scanned the room. We were backstage, minutes away from our close-out performance in Paris, France.

"We love you Parris," the band members and dancers cheered.

I fanned my face as my eyes watered. "I love you too." I took my finger and wiped the tears. "Stop it y'all."

We gave each other hugs and I watched them all go out onstage. Casper stood beside me. "This is your time baby. Do your thing." He leaned down and kissed me.

"Don't forget to come out onstage when I say your name," I said, as I wiped my lipstick from his lips.

"Parris, I told you I want to stay in the background," he protested.

Casper wouldn't admit it, but he liked being in the limelight just as much as he enjoyed making music. I saw how he shined when behind the camera. When I walked out onstage, I waved at the fans. They went wild. They chanted, "Parris. Parris."

"Thank you for welcoming me back to the city of love," I said, once I got the crowd to simmer down.

"We love you Parris," someone from the crowd screamed.

"And Parris loves you," I responded, as I blew a kiss in his direction.

The celebrities in attendance sat in a VIP section and they were singing and dancing along like the rest of the crowd. When we came to the final set, I called Casper out onstage for the last number. It was the remix version that would be released in video and on the radio the following week in the States.

"This is my boo," I said, as I held Casper's hand and led him onto the stage. He rapped his part to my new up-tempo song as I sang the hook, "This is my boo . . . this is how we do it."

We went back and forth and had the place rocking

from side to side. Before exiting the stage, Casper kissed me. The crowd went wild. I patted him on the butt as he left the stage. I yelled, "Now, that's my boo."

I thanked my band members, dancers, my mom, friends, and Casper. The sounds of the standing ovation imprinted in my mind had me riding on a cloud until the plane landed back in Los Angeles.

26

DOUBLE PLATINUM

"Looking good Parris," Sandy said, as she sat in the chair across from me.

It had been a week since my tour ended. I sat in Sparkie's. Carmen was late. Sandy was the last person I wanted to see. I rolled my eyes. "Sorry, that seat is taken."

"This won't take long. I wanted to give you a welcome home gift."

Before I could respond to her, Sandy slipped me a brown envelope and left the table. I opened it up and inside was a case with a DVD. The words written on the outside of it read, "For your eyes only."

"What is she up to?" I asked myself. I looked around the room in the direction she walked. She stood near the door. Our eyes locked. She smiled and as she turned to walk away she ran into Carmen. Carmen brushed her to the side. Sandy pointed in my direction. Carmen looked. I waved my hand in the air ignoring Sandy's friendly gesture.

"I almost forgot I was at Sparkie's when she stepped on my new shoes I got in Paris," Carmen said, while taking her seat.

"Sandy's like a wart. She shows up at wrong time," I said.

Carmen's phone rang. She prompted me to be quiet. "I'll be right back."

While waiting on Carmen, I took the envelope and pulled out the DVD again. I was staring at it, when Carmen returned. "What's that?" she asked.

I handed it to her. "Something my buddy Sandy gave me."

"Burn it. Don't even look at it," Carmen suggested.

"I haven't figured out what I'm going to do with it yet." I took it from her and threw it in my purse.

"The 'My Boo' video is number one on all the video stations, which leads me to why I called you here today," Carmen said, as I smiled thinking about all of the number one songs I've released from my CD. Carmen picked up her Blackberry. She continued to say, "More and more people want to see more of Parris; so I've got you a guest spot on Idol. You have a walk-in cameo in Martin's next film and let's see, Bruce wants you to read for his next action flick."

I didn't know what to say. Being back on top in music was enough for me. Being on TV, in films, acting; I hadn't thought of it. Other singers did both, so I guess it was about time I took it under consideration. I asked, "Will this interfere with my music?"

"If anything, it'll increase your record sales. In fact, right now there's a bidding war on who will get the next Parris CD."

"The record company is having a special celebration for me tonight. We'll see what happens." I leaned back and crossed my arms.

"Casper, can you pass me the lipstick that's in my brown bag?" I yelled from the bathroom.

"What?" he asked

"My brown bag, can you bring me the lipstick out of it," I shouted. I should have had my makeup artist here tonight, but didn't.

Casper handed me my makeup bag. He held the DVD in his hand. "What's this?"

"Something some reporter gave me," I responded as I removed items looking for my coral brown lipstick.

"What's on it?" he asked.

"I don't know. I haven't had time to watch it," I said, trying not to get irritated. I located the lipstick and put on my finishing touches.

I brushed past him to finish getting dressed. "How do I look?" I asked, as I admired the form-fitting burgundy skirt and off-white silk shirt and matching jacket.

Casper responded, "Great as usual."

After trying on several different pairs of shoes, I found a pair that went perfectly with the outfit. I squeezed my feet in them and met Casper downstairs.

"I'm sleeping with a star," Casper teased me later on that night while we were snuggled up in bed.

"A double-platinum star at that baby," I said, as he tickled me.

He had me pinned under him. "I told you this CD would be a hit."

I smiled. "Thanks to you."

"With a voice like yours, you would have gone double platinum regardless," he said, before leaning down to kiss me.

In between kisses, I said, "I wouldn't want to share the honors with anyone else but you."

He got up to turn out the light. I glanced at the glass-framed award the record company gave me showcasing my new double-platinum status in record sales. I've gone gold and I've gone platinum, but for this album to go double platinum in record time, it was phenomenal.

"I see some doubles I want to play with right now," Casper said, as he pulled the covers off exposing my breasts.

"You're bad."

In his best MJ impression, he said, "And you know it."

The following morning, I did radio interviews with all of the national syndicated morning shows. I thanked the hosts and their listening audience for making my reentry better than I could have imagined. So much had happened. The acting opportunities; my CD going double platinum. Life couldn't be better.

Later that day, Casper and I lounged on the sofa. Casper fed me a spoonful of strawberry ice cream. "Are you ready to set a date?" he asked.

I replied, "Valentine's Day." I took the spoon from him and licked both sides of it. I noticed the bulge in his pants as I licked.

"I don't think Valentine's is on a Saturday, dear," he responded. He took the spoon away from me and dipped it back into the ice cream. "You better be glad I don't mind your germs."

"Out with the tradition. I want our day to be on the national day for lovers." I got up to go look for a calendar. I flipped the pages. "It's a Thursday."

"But what about our guests? Wouldn't that be inconsiderate?" That's what I liked about Casper. He was always thinking about other people.

"I'm sure if we tell people now, they can make the appropriate arrangements," I responded.

He pulled me onto his lap. "February the fourteenth it is."

The following week, Casper and I were scheduled to perform my latest single "My Boo" on 106 and Park. The hosts kept us laughing and by the time I took the stage, I felt like I was at a small house party instead of being on TV. The video for my other single "Try Me" remained number one for so long, they had to retire it to give other videos a chance.

"Hailey's on the phone. She wants to know if we're ready to officially announce our wedding date." Casper asked me, as he pulled his car into his parking garage.

"Sure," I responded.

He followed me into the house. I disarmed the alarm as he finished his conversation with Hailey. He disconnected the call and said, "She says thanks and she can't wait. She's going to start the promo running immediately."

I helped Casper pack for his trip. "How long will

you be gone this time?" I asked, as I folded up his boxers and placed them in his bag.

"Only a few days. After your tour, I promised to never be away from you for long," he stated.

People were surprised that although we both had money, we didn't act like the typical stars with all the assistants and huge entourages. Casper said it best one night when we were having dinner with Mason and her husband. "I don't pay for friends and it only takes one person to do one task." I agreed. I could stand to cut back some of my expenses, but compared to others, I don't think I wasted money. My mom disagreed.

I dropped Casper off at the airport. "Behave," I said.

"I need to be telling you that," Casper responded as he hugged and kissed me.

The person pulling her car behind mine blew her horn. "Whatever," I said, as I got back into my car and drove off.

I talked to Casper on my cell phone until he boarded his plane.

27

MY LIFE

Now that Casper was gone, I was bored. When I'm bored or upset, I clean. I started going through my purses. I came across the DVD Sandy had given me a few weeks ago. I could hear Carmen's voice in my head saying throw it away, but I was curious. I found the remote and switched it to DVD mode. I placed the DVD in and sat on the edge of the bed. Sandy's voice is heard in the intro.

"Parris and Casper, Hollywood's hottest couple, have been together for over a year now. Many of you saw the rock on her hand in interviews. But what you don't know is . . ."

The phone rang. I pressed the pause button. I answered the phone. Mason and I talked until I heard the TV blasting. The pause only lasted so long before clicking off the DVD player. "Girl, I forgot I was watching something when you called." The phone beeped.

"Anyway, that's Casper. I'll call you later," I said, while clicking over to talk to Casper.

"Miss me yet?" he asked.

"You know I do," I responded.

With the time difference, I didn't want to keep him on the phone long since I knew he had an early morning recording session. As soon as we hung up, I clicked the PLAY button on the DVD.

Sandy's commentary continued. "Warning. What you're about to see may be explicit. So if you have sensitive eyes, now is the time to turn it off."

"This woman is crazy." I blurted.

Of course by now, my interests are piqued so I continued to watch. The camera showed men in a room filled with naked strippers. They were hollering and throwing dollars while the women performed tricks that left my mouth wide open. I recognized a few of the faces. Some were rappers and a few producers I had worked with in the past. I gasped. The camera zoomed in as one stripper grinded her pantyless hips on the lap of Casper. I hit the rewind button several times as I saw Casper enjoying the performance. I cursed out loud. Sandy's commentary continued. "Check out the woman in the red as she performs."

Although the camera zoomed in, you couldn't see exactly what she was doing. Her head was in a position that left no doubts what act she was performing. I couldn't believe Casper would participate in something as scandalous as this. And the fact that Sandy had a video made it even more sickening.

What made me continue to watch the video, I don't know. I was stunned. The camera moved back to where Casper was sitting and I threw the remote on the bed when I saw this other woman performing the same act on him as the woman in the red. Casper's head was thrown back so I couldn't see his facial expression, but from the sounds he was making, he seemed to be enjoying it.

"How could you?" I repeated over and over as tears flowed down my face.

Sandy's commentary said, "Only two people have a copy. You and me. Call me."

The screen faded to black.

"Lord, what am I to do? I loved him. I thought he was the one. Why me?" I questioned.

I didn't know what to do. I don't know how long I sat on the edge of the bed curled up in a ball rocking back and forth. I fell down on top of the covers and rocked myself to sleep. When I awoke the next morning and looked in the mirror, my eyes were puffy and red. I tried clearing them with eye drops but it only irritated them. Even the long bath I took didn't ease the pain.

I didn't know what to do. I didn't know who to call. Carmen was my friend but she was dating Casper's brother. Mason was probably sleeping because she's on the graveyard shift this week. I wouldn't dare tell my mama about this. The only person I could think of was Rose.

Oh my goodness, before calling Rose, I had to call Hailey and stop her from running those promo ads. "Hailey, I hope I caught you in time," I said, sounding out of breath.

"We're in a meeting now, but when I saw your number flash, I answered."

"The dates changed and, well . . . I'd rather not go into it right now, but next week is not a good time," I stuttered.

"Are you okay?" Hailey asked.

"Yes. No. Never mind. I got to go," I said, hanging up before I blurted out why it would be a cold day in hell before I married Casper. In fact, I needed to call Hailey back to let her know that. Before I could dial her number, the devil himself called.

"Don't ever call me again," I answered and clicked the phone off.

He called right back. I heard him say, "Parris." I clicked.

This time he called the house phone. "Stop calling me," I yelled through the phone.

"Why you tripping?" Casper asked.

"Tripping. Ask your trick!" I yelled before slamming the phone so hard it fell off the bed.

Casper continued to call me throughout the day, but I didn't accept any of his calls. I avoided everybody's calls because I wasn't in the mood to deal with this. Casper sent a courier over with a note. I read it and tore it up. I thought another courier was outside, so when I heard a knock on the door, I wasn't expecting to see Sandy standing on the other side.

I held the doorknob. My head moved as I said, "Excuse me if I don't invite you in."

"Have you seen the video?" she asked with a smug look on her face.

"All I want to know is why do you have it in for me?"

Sandy appeared to be thrown back with my question. She attempted to walk through the door, but I moved my body to block her. "You're not welcome here."

She took a few steps back. She fanned right above her nose. "Dear, there's a thing such as mouthwash. And your hair. With all the money you have, you can afford a hairstylist."

Sandy stood far enough out the door that when I

slammed it, it didn't hit her in the face. Although it would have made me feel better if it did, I didn't need a lawsuit on my hands.

The doorbell rang. "Go away," I yelled.

"We need to talk. I promise, it'll only take a few minutes," Sandy said.

"Dang, she will not give up." I walked back to the door and opened it.

"All I'm asking for is an exclusive," Sandy stated.

I threw up my middle finger. "There, you got it," I said.

I closed the door, but this time Sandy put her foot in the way to block. "Ouch," she screamed.

"If you agree, I won't show the video," she said.

I laughed. "It wasn't me on the screen, so have at it."

"But, I need you. My job's in jeopardy if you don't give me this interview."

With her admission, I opened the door back up. "You need me. Hmm," I said, as I placed my index finger on my face near my lips.

"All I need for you to do is answer a few questions and then I'll give you the original," she stated.

I threw my hands in the air. "What? My life is an open book. I have no privacy because of people like you. What do you want to know?"

"Can I come in?" she asked.

By now I'm calmer. I thought about it. "You might as well because I see you're not going away."

I led her into my living room. She looked around as we walked. She bent down to touch one of my figurines. "Don't touch," I snapped.

She looked at me and stood back up and followed me to the couch.

"I have a few questions for *you*," I said.

"Anything you want," she responded.

"Where did you get the video?"

"A friend." She tapped her fingers on her leg.

"What do you plan on doing with the video?" I asked.

"Nothing. If you cooperate," Sandy responded. Now she's looking me square in the eyes.

"Like I said, you showing that tape has nothing to do with me."

She looked down at my ring. "I'm sure you don't want the world to know your fiancé is out messing around."

I turned the ring around on my finger. "What Casper does is his business and none of yours."

"Besides an exclusive, I could use a few extra dollars to help me with a few bills," she stated.

I laughed. "You are something else."

She looked around the room. "With your comeback you don't want your rep tarnished."

"Not to sound like a broken record, but that video has nothing to do with me." I stood up and continued to say, "I think it's time that you leave."

She reached into her pocket and handed me a card. "If you change your mind, call me. If I don't hear from you, I'll share the video with the highest bidder."

I didn't have to kick her out, because she voluntarily left. The door clicked. I locked the door and slid down the doorway crying. I put on a strong front in front of her, but inside I was crying. I couldn't believe Casper would do this to me. I would be publicly humiliated. How could I marry a man who had no respect me, for us, for our future? If I would have kept him at a distance, my heart wouldn't be breaking in two.

I got up. I needed to pull myself together. I avoided everyone all day. I had been putting off calling Carmen since I found out last night, but now I had no choice. I wasn't agreeing to any of Sandy's terms so I'm sure the video would be surfacing soon. Carmen agreed to meet me at my place as soon as she could.

I went to the kitchen to fix something to eat, but everything I picked up in the refrigerator turned my stomach. The stress was too much. Not only did I lose my man, I've lost my appetite. I wanted to lose more weight, but not like this. Juice was the only thing that seemed appealing. I poured a huge glass and drank it nonstop.

What I really needed was a real drink. I went to the bar and poured myself a shot of tequila. It was the wrong decision because a few minutes later, I stood over a toilet throwing it up along with the remnants of my near-empty stomach.

I washed my mouth out, brushed my teeth and gargled with mouthwash. I pulled my hair back into a ponytail and waited downstairs for Carmen to arrive. Of course she was tied to the phone when she arrived. She hugged me. She followed me to the living room as she finished her conversation.

"Looks like I have an emergency," she stated to whomever was on the phone.

I flipped stations on the TV. I ended up on one of the music channels. They were showing the video of "My Boo." Casper was doing his part. I clicked the OFF button.

"I still can't believe that bastard," I blurted.

Carmen ended her call and said, "What did he do?"

"Oh, he didn't do anything. That's the problem," I responded.

I explained to her what I saw on the video and Sandy's visit. Carmen sat in disbelief. "Do you still have the video?"

"It's on the floor in my bedroom if you want to see it."

She went upstairs to retrieve it. She walked back in the room and said, "Do you mind?"

I threw her the remote. "Be my guest. I'll be in the den when you finish."

I couldn't stomach to see it again. I'd watched it enough last night. I turned on my computer and checked my message board. Hearing what my fans had to say is what I needed to put me in a better mood. My e-mail was filled with messages from Casper. I deleted them all without opening them. Carmen came in the room cursing like a sailor. "I'm going to kill him," she said.

"Stand in line," I responded, turning off the monitor and swivelling the chair around to face Carmen.

She threw the disc on the desk. "What does he have to say about this mess?"

"I don't know. I haven't talked to him."

"What? If that were my man, I would be all up in his face."

"He's in New York and won't be back until tomorrow night."

"I need to make some phone calls. His dirt will not be reflected on you dear. You can believe that."

Carmen and I switched seats. I thumbed through a fashion magazine as she typed something on the computer and talked on her phone. "She's sitting right here, but has no comment right now," she stated.

The printer automatically turned itself on as the paper went through it. Carmen picked it up and handed it to me. I read it. "Parris Mitchell regrets to say her engagement to Casper Johnson has been postponed. She appreciates your concerns, but she will be taking the next few weeks to deal with the change."

I handed it back to her and said, "Sounds good to me."

"So when are you going to break the news to Casper?"

"Let him be surprised. Oh, do me a favor." I removed the ring he gave me and handed it to Carmen. "Tell him, he can give it to the trick in the video."

I was too upset to talk to Carmen anymore. I left her in the den doing what she does and left to go take a long bath. Carmen was gone when I got back downstairs. She left the ring with a note. "Maybe you two can work it out."

"Not," I said. I balled the paper up and threw it in the trash.

28

BUDDY

My phone rang off the hook the next day when reports of my broken engagement hit the papers and the entertainment shows. I refused to answer my phone. I spoke with my mom to warn her and Mason. Mason attempted to convince me to talk it over with Casper, but she was too late. Carmen had already faxed over my statement to the wire service, so now Casper and I were on the tips of everybody's tongues.

My heart ached for Casper, but I couldn't see being with him after the video. I was drying off my hair and entering my bedroom, when the sight of Casper sitting on the bed startled me. He was holding several papers. He threw them at me.

His eyes were watery and red. "When I got to the studio this morning, people were apologizing and saying how sorry they were about us." My feet felt glued to the floor. I stood there and listened as he said, "I didn't have a clue on what they were talking about.

Big showed me the article in the *Daily.* I felt like someone stabbed me in the heart when I read the announcement. I called you, but you didn't answer your phone."

Casper looked as if he was on the verge of opening the floodgates of his tears. A part of me felt bad. I said, "Sorry you had to find out about it that way, but you weren't here."

"I thought I knew you," Casper said. He stood up and walked toward me. I moved back. He said, "Don't worry. I'm not going to lay hands on you. I feel like it right now, but after all of this, I still love you."

When he got to the door, he turned around and asked, "Why Parris? Why?"

"Follow me," I said. He did as I commanded. He followed me around the house as I retrieved the scratched DVD and placed it in the DVD player. I hit the PLAY button. "This is why!" I threw the remote at him. It hit him on the chest before hitting the floor.

I ran back upstairs and slammed my bedroom door and locked it. A few minutes later, Casper attempted to turn the knob but it wouldn't budge. He knocked on the door and yelled, "Open the door Parris."

"Get the hell out of my house," I yelled.

He begged. "I can explain the video."

"I'm sure you can. But guess what, baby, I don't care! Leave me alone," I yelled through the door.

"Now it all makes sense. Baby, we can work it out."

"Go away Casper. It's o-v-e-r."

He attempted to convince me to open the door so we could talk face-to-face. I refused. After thirty minutes or so, he got tired. I heard the front door slam. I rushed to the bedroom window and watched him get into his car. I also saw cameras flashing.

The following morning, a picture of Casper storming

away hit the front page of the entertainment section. Xavier called trying to plead Casper's case but I wasn't hearing him.

"If you want to continue to talk, don't mention your brother to me," I stated.

Carmen called me upset shortly thereafter. "Now, Parris, I know you're going through something right now, but there's no need to treat everybody else with no respect."

"Yada yada," I stated.

"Check your attitude," Carmen said.

I contemplated on coming back with a response, but instead I said, "I got to go." I hung up because if the conversation would have gone any further, I probably would have lost a best friend and an agent.

The situation with Casper wrecked havoc in my life in so many ways. I couldn't turn on the television without hearing about our breakup. I didn't dare watch videos, because if it wasn't my video, I would see him in a video with some of the other artists he'd helped produce. Everything I watched reminded me of him.

The next few weeks flew by. I lost more weight because every time I tried to eat something, it would come back up. My nerves were shot beyond belief. I needed to schedule a doctor's appointment because my antidepressant pill supply was getting low. With all the drama, I needed something to help me cope.

Hailey called me a few times wanting to know if I wanted to come on her show and tell my side of the story. She insisted she wouldn't allow her friendship with Casper to interfere with her questioning. I could tell she was lying, so I declined. To my surprise, she did offer some words of encouragement. "If you need to talk off the record, I'm only a phone call away."

I thanked her but knew I would rather talk to Sandy Blair than talk to her. They both were cut from the same cloth—cutthroat.

An assistant had been working overtime to respond to phone calls and e-mails. I didn't want to talk to anyone unless it was my mom, Mason, or Carmen. Casper called, e-mailed me, sent flowers, and sent messages via Carmen. I ignored them all. Several award shows were coming up and I was scheduled to perform. I spent my free time rehearsing and trying to block out my feelings for Casper. I wasn't successful at all. While walking from a meeting with a movie producer, I ran into Trevon, one of the sexiest actors on the West Coast. His skin was the color of dark brown sugar and as smooth as a new leather belt.

We exchanged numbers, although a part of me felt guilty giving another man my number. Who I was fooling? With all of the women who couldn't wait to put their claws into Casper, I'm sure he had already moved on. Trevon called me every night but I refused to go out with him. He insisted he only wanted friendship from me and wanted me to loosen up around him. I couldn't because I didn't want to take the chance that I could actually like someone else other than Casper.

One night I was surfing the Internet and talking to Trevon at the same time when I came across a snippet of that nasty video with Casper and the strippers. I used the search engine and put Casper's name in it and saw that the video was just leaked. "Now the whole world knows," I said. I explained to Trevon my discovery.

"Don't you think you're being too hard on him?" he asked.

"Uh, no," I responded.

"Give the man another chance. We do make mistakes," Trevon said. I listened to him go on and on as he pled Casper's case.

"Are you going to be my date for the awards show or not?" I blurted; anything to shut him up about Casper.

"I'll be honored. What should I wear?" he asked, sounding like a woman.

I laughed. "I'm sure you'll find something appropriate."

We talked until we both got sleepy. I realized I didn't have any romantic feelings toward Trevon. I put him in the buddy category and from how he was talking to me about Casper; I assumed he put me in the friend category too.

29

TRY ME

Mason was upset to learn that Trevon was going to be my escort to the BEAM awards. I didn't tell Carmen, because I knew she would tell Xavier and somehow it would get back to Casper. Trevon's coming with me was more of a publicity stunt. He knew walking in with me would gain him more media attention.

As an awards presenter and performer, I spent the morning of the awards show rehearsing. I was asked to be on several morning shows. I garnered the sympathy of many of the anchors because the video of Casper leaking around awards time was a hot topic. Most anchors avoided bringing his name up. When questions arose about him, I responded, "No comment."

Carmen waited for me near the limousine after my last interview. "Word is out you're bringing a date tonight," she blurted without even a hello.

The limousine driver opened the door. "You coming or not?" I asked, as I stepped in.

"I have my own car. What were you thinking?"

"When you can come to me as my friend instead of my agent, then we can talk. Otherwise, I'm pressed for time. See you."

The limousine driver shut the door. I made sure the doors were locked. I didn't feel like dealing with Carmen and her attitude. I needed a friend and thus far Mason and Trevon were the only two people who really listened to how I was feeling.

I had my hairdresser and makeup artist meet me at my house. I wore a dress from Fazio's Rose Petal collection. I put on a girdle to hold in my stomach because although I was losing weight, my stomach poked out a little. The red sequined dress with the low neckline felt like a second skin. Once I was fully dressed, I gave my stylist strict instructions on what to bring for my performance.

Trevon picked me up in a long black stretch limousine. He wore a simple yet elegant black tuxedo with red cummerbund. "Let's make some people jealous," he whispered in my ear, as we exited the limousine in front of the Staples Center.

Cameras flashed and reporters bombarded us with many questions. "Are you two dating now?" "Trevon, are you the real reason why Parris left Casper?" "Parris, did you know about the stripper tape before you broke up with Casper?"

My head was spinning. If Trevon hadn't been standing there to hold me up, I would have fallen. I didn't know which way to go. Trevon glided me over to where we were to take our standard publicity photos. Photographers took pictures of me by myself and then some with Trevon. I knew it was customary to do interviews, so I did them only with the reporters I had respect for.

"What are you singing tonight?" Hailey asked, as special correspondent for one of the big three entertainment shows.

"You'll have to watch to find out," I responded, as Trevon and I continued down the red carpet.

To my surprise, Sandy was also working as a correspondent with one of the big three networks. I guess the videotape did somebody some good. She stuck the microphone in my face. I wanted to punch her, but instead I put on a fake smile. "Have you run into Casper yet? I heard he's here somewhere," Sandy stated.

"I'm sure he is." I continued to smile. Anyone watching could tell it was fake. Sandy's cameraman attempted to direct her to another singer.

I walked up to where Trevon stood. "I'm ready to go inside," I said. I had to repeat myself because of the noise level.

"I saw Casper," Trevon said, once we got inside.

"I heard he was here," I stated.

"Does he know you're here with me?" Trevon asked.

Casper said, "I do now."

I turned around and saw the look of disappointment on Casper's face. I wanted to explain that there wasn't anything going on with Trevon, but my pride got in the way. Instead I said, "Hi, Casper."

He ignored me. Carmen looked at me and shook her head. Xavier mouthed the word, "Why?" and went to console his brother. Trevon and I stood watching them go by. I'm not sure if anyone else saw the awkward moment. My feelings of sympathy for Casper didn't last long. Casper had his nerve to be upset at me after the mess I saw on that video.

While they went to take their seats, I went backstage to my dressing room to freshen up. "What are you doing?" Casper asked, after coming in and closing the door.

I rolled my eyes. "Leave please."

He walked closer to me and said, "I can't believe you're cheating on me."

I held my hand up and switched it from side to side. "News flash. We're not together anymore."

Casper pulled me into his arms and kissed me. My mouth opened automatically and my body unwillingly responded. My heart fluttered. He said, "You'll always be mine."

He left me in the room in a daze. Someone stuck their head through the doorway and said, "You're on in five."

I looked in the mirror to freshen up and went onstage to present the Best New R & B Male Singer award.

Afterward, I took a seat on the front row next to Trevon. He held my hand for support as my name was called among the other nominees for Best Dance Song—"My Boo." Trevon had to nudge me to go onstage when they called my name. I was so excited, I almost tripped going on the stage. A few people laughed. I didn't have an acceptance speech prepared, so I ad-libbed. "I want to thank God for granting me this songbird voice. I want to thank my parents for always believing in me. My family. My friends. And the man who used to be my boo."

I held the award up in the air and walked backstage to go take pictures. Tears flowed down my face because I wished I could have been sharing this moment with Casper. "Pull yourself together," I told myself.

Before I could go back to my seat, it was announced I won another award. When I went to accept, Casper stood at the podium. We won the award for Best Collaboration. He kissed me on the cheek when I walked up. I plastered on a smile and took my award. I kept the acceptance speech short this time.

He placed his hand on my back as we walked off-stage, but I increased my pace and I could only feel the tips of his fingers at that point. We took pictures and I sped away to the dressing room to change into my performance outfit.

Fortunately, when I went to the side of the stage, Casper's was nowhere to be seen. The lights dimmed. The curtain that was shaped like a raindrop opened and I walked out singing, "You don't have to be lonely . . . Only if you want to be . . . You don't have to be lonely . . . You can just call me . . ."

As I scanned the crowd, my eyes locked with Casper's. For those brief moments, I was singing the song to him. When the band started playing the music for the song "Try Me," I removed my jacket. My dancers and I had the audience on their feet. I ended the routine by blowing a kiss out to the audience.

I changed back into the dress I originally wore so I could go take my seat. As I walked back to my seat, people were telling me how well I performed. Casper nodded his head to agree but didn't say anything. I sat down by Trevon and listened for the other winners. When the nominees for Best Female R & B singer/group was announced, I didn't think I would win. When I heard my name called, I jumped up for joy.

"Once again, without God, I wouldn't be here. To my family, my friends. My record label for giving me this last shot. To my super producer. To my fans, this one's for you." I kissed it and held it up in the air.

The comedian Sandbag joked, "She might as well stay on the stage, because she's running this shindig tonight."

The crowd laughed. While I was backstage having my

picture taken, they announced the Best R & B song. Sandbag grabbed me. "Go get your award girl."

I walked back onstage. "Thank you all again. This has been an incredible night. A night I'll never forget. God bless."

The award for Best R & B album was up. I had a feeling I was going to win it too, but didn't want to get my hopes up. "Parris," Rose announced.

I hugged Rose. She whispered, "Congratulations girl. You deserve it."

With tears streaming down my face, I held the award tight. "Praise God. It's been a trying year, but this goes to show you that in spite of everything, you still can achieve. Just don't give up."

I thanked everybody I may have forgotten earlier. I walked backstage and went through the interviews and pictures. Many of the celebrities mingled backstage long after the awards show ended. Last year I didn't attend any of the parties, but this year I planned on hitting as many as I could. Tonight was my night and I planned on partying until I dropped. I found Trevon and we party-hopped. We saved the best party for last. The one where the purple one himself was hosting. It was "the party" as far as anyone in the industry was concerned.

The doorman checked for our names on the list and allowed us in. The place was already jumping when we arrived. The purple one was onstage performing. We made it just in time. "Tre, don't let me stop you from doing your thing. I'm all right," I said, as he left me to mingle.

I hugged and kissed people as I made my way closer to the front. "Ladies and gentlemen, here's Parris. Parris, come up here and let us here you blow."

I couldn't believe he was calling me onstage. He

started singing one of his classics and then he gave me the microphone. I got into it as I spit out verse after verse. The people danced and clapped and I hugged him before exiting the stage. After winning all of those awards, I didn't think the night could have gotten any better. To sing with one of my idols; well that was the pinnacle.

I danced with several different people. I ran into Trevon a few times and each time he was with a different woman. I assured him I was fine on my own. My fingers touched my lips. I recalled the kiss from earlier.

"Your date seems to be preoccupied," Casper whispered in my ear from behind. I could smell the alcohol on his breath. I attempted to move, but couldn't because we were standing in a congested area.

"You're a borderline stalker," I responded and turned. When I turned, I was right on Casper's chest. I was about to say something else, when Rose and Lance walked up.

"Are you two back together yet?" Rose blurted.

Lance hit her arm. "Lance, I hope you're driving, because Rose sounds like she's been drinking," I said, as I moved away to get some air.

"You can't run forever," Casper yelled as I made my way through the crowd. I made it outside of the door. I bent down to catch my breath. When I looked up, Sandy was there with a microphone.

I wasn't in the mood to deal with her, so I ignored her. I didn't know where Trevon was but I was ready to go. The limousine could come back to pick him up. I saw our driver outside and directed him to take me home. Once I arrived home, he helped me bring in my awards. "You can sit them on the couch," I stated. I handed him a hundred dollar tip and locked up.

Trevon called me on the cell. "I was looking for you but that reporter told me you had left. You all right?" he slurred.

"I'm fine. The driver is on his way back to pick you up."

"I'll call him. I won't be going home. I'm going to another party." I heard some woman call his name in the background. He continued to say, "I'll call you later. I'm coming baby." He hung up.

"Looks like we both were winners tonight. Trevon and his new conquest and me and my many awards," I said to myself.

30

I LOVE YOU

I took a nap because I wanted to watch some of the morning shows. Fortunately, they interviewed me before I left the Staples Center because otherwise, I would have been too tired to talk. I laid in bed and flipped from station to station.

"Did Parris leave playboy Casper Johnson, who's also known as CJ the Hitmaker, over stripper videotape," the SBC news anchorwoman said, before highlighting an edited version of the videotape.

By now I'm sitting straight up in the bed. The anchorwoman continues to talk. "The best revenge is to win—Parris Mitchell walked away with eight awards." Video clips of me walking to accept award after award played.

"Marie Scandovia is on a fight for women's rights in the music business. Marie, what do you think about the video?"

"It sickens me to see it. CJ and the others in the video need to be held accountable for their actions." Marie looked directly in the camera and said, "If you're one of the women in the video, my organization WAIJ-Women Against InJustice, pleads for you to contact us at 1-888-555-WAIJ."

Although I was mad at Casper for cheating on me, it upset me to see Maria Scandovia and so many others condemn him. Those women in the video knew what they were doing. No one put a gun up to their heads and made them do what they did. As a woman, I thought we all needed to start having more respect for ourselves and refrain from doing degrading acts. I understood those women probably needed the money, but still, it didn't look like anyone forced them to perform. The more money thrown their way, the more they performed.

I flipped off the television and slid back under the covers. The excitement from my big night made me feel like Cinderella after the ball. In the morning hours, the video fiasco seemed to piggyback off my winnings. I don't know how long I had been sleeping, but when I awoke, I almost had a heart attack when I saw Casper sitting in the chaise watching me. He looked bad. His eyes were bloodshot. I shot up and said, "What are you doing here?"

"I needed to make sure you were fine. I called you and knocked."

I looked at the clock and it was almost two in the afternoon. I didn't realize I had slept that long. "I was sleeping."

He remained seated and said, "So you haven't heard?"

"If you're talking about the video leaking. I've heard. I've seen it." I stopped in midsentence because at that moment, I forgot about being mad at him for cheating on me. I wanted to comfort him. I wanted to erase the pain I saw seeping from his eyes.

Casper wobbled over to the bed. He reeked of alcohol. I had never seen him drunk—this was a first for me. "Parris, I need you."

He fell on the bed on top of me. I pushed him to the side. "I'm calling Xavier."

I reached for the telephone. Casper swung his arm over mine and I lost my grip on the receiver. It fell to the floor. He said, "I was young. I was stupid."

I waited for him to finish but instead I heard him start snoring. I removed his arm from around me and shook him. "Wake up."

He didn't budge. I picked up the phone receiver on the floor and dialed Xavier's cell phone number. I was upset and started spouting out, "I could have him arrested for breaking and entering."

Xavier interrupted. "Where's my brother now?"

I stood and walked toward the bathroom, because the stench was beginning to make me queasy. "He's straddled his funky behind on my bed. You need to come get him."

Xavier assured me he would be there as soon as possible. In the meantime, I sprayed almost a full can of air freshener to cover up the alcohol smell. I heard him call my name out in his sleep.

"Disgusting," was all I could muster up to say.

By the time I showered and dressed, Xavier and Carmen were downstairs. I welcomed them through the door with open arms. "He's still upstairs," I said, pointing.

Xavier left to check on his brother. Carmen looked at me. She and I weren't on the best of terms, but we both forgot that as we hugged each other. "How are you holding up?" Carmen asked.

I wiped my eyes with my right hand. "I'm not falling apart if that's what you're worried about."

I moved to go up the stairway. By now, Xavier was walking back down. "He'll be all right. He's in the shower."

"Let me go see if I can find something for him to put on," I said, as I walked past Xavier.

I went to one of the guest bedroom closets where Casper kept some of his clothes. Although we had broken up, I hadn't thought about his clothes being here because I hardly used the room. Shoot, the maid service people could have hidden some things in here and I wouldn't have known. The small walk-in closet overflowed with his stuff. It looked as if he were moving in on the sly. I grabbed a pair of jeans and a button-down shirt. He's such a neat freak. He had boxers hung up on a few hangers. I grabbed a pair of those.

The water was still running in the bathroom when I walked in. I laid the clothes on the bed and waited for him to exit. He took so long I thought I would have to go rescue him. One towel was wrapped around Casper's waist. He rubbed his head with another towel. He jumped when he saw me sitting on the bed. I guess he didn't expect to see me. He looked away embarrassed. I handed him his boxers. He turned to walk back into the bathroom when I said, "It's not like I haven't see you naked before."

He stopped and I had a beautiful view of what I had been missing. I wasn't going to give him the satisfaction of seeing how much I still wanted him in that way, so I turned my head. Casper dressed in record time. I followed him downstairs.

Carmen rushed over to Casper and hugged him. A twinge of jealousy went through my body. "Don't you ever scare us like that again," Carmen said.

Xavier said, "Now that I know you're all right, we're leaving."

I looked between Carmen and Xavier. I said, "What? He needs to go with you."

Carmen rushed by my side. She looped her arm through mine as she prodded me to walk towards the kitchen. "You guys need to talk. You won't listen to me, so at least hear him out."

I turned around and saw Xavier hug his brother. "I've never seen him like this," I said.

"He's been miserable without you," Carmen stated as we waited on the sidelines until it appeared Casper had pulled himself together.

"There's nothing he can say. He cheated. He got caught and now the whole world knows. I'm sorry he was exposed like that, but I'm the victim in all of this," I said, as we walked back toward the foyer.

"Listen to him," Carmen said, as she went by Xavier's side. "I'm ready."

Xavier looked at Casper. "You going to be all right man?"

Casper nodded his head up and down. He looked at me and back at Xavier. "It's cool."

I stood with my arms crossed as I watched Casper walk to the kitchen. "You're lucky I haven't kicked you out, but it doesn't give you free reign to go all over my house," I said, as I picked up my pace and walked behind him.

He went to the refrigerator and opened it. I closed it. "I'm hungry and you look like you haven't eaten in weeks," he said, as he waited for me to move.

"There're several Mickey D's on your way home," I responded, not moving.

Casper reached one arm up over my head and leaned closer. "I don't want to fight with you anymore."

"Ugh. I'm moving," I said, as I slipped from under him. "You might want to gargle some more because your breath is kicking."

He laughed. A laugh I had been missing. "That's the kindest thing you've said to me today."

I sat on the bar stool and watched him take food out the refrigerator. "I do think better on a full stomach."

While he cooked two omelettes, I read the paper. I pretended to read. It was hard concentrating. I should still be mad at him, but something he said earlier stuck with me. He mentioned about being young. I would ask him what he meant after breakfast. I set the table in the kitchen while he finished cooking.

Before eating, Casper reached for my hand to say grace. I pulled away, but when I saw the look in his eyes, I placed my hand on top of his. We bowed our heads as he prayed. We ate the majority of our meal in silence. He watched me and I watched him. I had plenty of unanswered questions, I decided now was the time to ask. I had no plans of being this close to him again, so I might as well make the best use of this time we were spending together.

"Why did you do it?" I asked, while taking a sip of my juice.

Barely above a whisper, Casper responded, "When I was younger, I did stupid things. My boys were doing it and at twenty-one, I just went along with the program."

I clapped my hands. "How long did it take you to come up with that lie?"

"All of this could have been avoided if you would have come to me," he stated, not addressing my last question.

By now, I'm on my feet. "You know what? It's time for you to leave. You're sober and you have an attitude."

Casper remained seated. "I'll leave when I say what I came here to say."

I crossed my arms and tapped my left foot. I looked at the clock on the wall. "You have five minutes."

"The video was altered. The person who altered it will be brought up on criminal charges. Your reporter friend, well she'll be dealt with too."

"I hear you."

"I love you and probably always will. I know now that what happened between us didn't have anything to do with a video. It was more about trust. And from how you handled it, it's something we never had."

He stood up and kissed me on the forehead and said, "Bye, Parris."

I didn't say a word; instead I watched the man I love walk out my front door. When my mind comprehended what he told me, when I realized that the video was filmed before we were together, when I realized I had made a mistake, I ran to the door. There was no sign of Casper. He was gone. I slammed the door and screamed, "No!"

31

LAST NIGHT

I called Mason. She sounded sluggish. When she realized it was me, she perked up. "Congrats on the awards. I had to work, but I kept the TV on, and I'm so proud of you," she blurted, not giving me a chance to get a word in.

"Thanks, but that's not why I'm calling," I said, in between tears. I explained to her the events following the awards ceremony.

"That's a relief. Now you two can move on," Mason commented.

I twirled my hair as I crossed my legs and sat farther back on the couch. "I don't think so. His good-bye seemed final."

Mason laughed. I didn't find anything funny. "Do you actually think he would go through all of that to tell you good-bye?"

"I don't know what to think," I admitted.

"He's hurting. You're hurting. You guys just need to figure out a way to work it out."

"Up until today, I didn't want to work it out," I stated.

Mason's last words to me before hanging up were, "Now that you do, what are you going to do about it?"

I called Carmen. "Sorry for how I've been acting lately," I said, while I still had courage to apologize.

"I apologize too for not being a better friend," she responded.

We went back and forth for a few minutes until we both agreed to forgive each other and not look back. "Casper's here," Carmen said.

I wanted to talk to him, but the way he walked out on me, I felt he should be the one to come to me. "And?"

"I overheard him tell Xavier about the altered video."

"It doesn't change anything," I said, sounding defeated.

"It could if you wanted it to. Stop being so stubborn," Carmen berated me.

I wanted Casper to come back to me on his own and without any interference. I didn't feel like I had to beg him. "He knows where to find me," I said as the tears streamed down my face.

The next voice I heard on the phone was Casper's. After I heard him say, "Hello," I hung up. "That was stupid," I said out loud.

I needed music. I placed one of my favorite CDs on the stereo. I glanced at my appearance and saw the huge contrast from last night. Last night I was glamorous, but today I looked a hot mess. The antidepressant medicine bottle in my purse was empty. I threw it in the trash and tossed and turned the entire night.

After a restless night of sleep, I checked my messages.

Surprisingly, I heard from a lot of people, but not one message from Casper. I called and made a doctor's appointment. I showered and dressed within an hour. Feeling jittery, I grabbed my keys and headed out the door. If I didn't make my doctor's appointment at ten, I would have to wait two days and I didn't think I could last two days without my pills.

The doctor's office was packed. I tried to stay anonymous but the clerk working the front desk kept making a scene. She wanted to take a picture with me. She insisted that I sign her CD, that she so happened to go to her car and get while I was waiting. I smiled and did it, although it irritated me that she was putting me on the spot. I didn't make it a habit of getting folks fired, but this was ridiculous. There should be some protocol. A professional she was not.

"Ms. Mitchell," a nurse, wearing a greenish blue uniform, came to the door and said.

I followed her into a room. I stepped on the scale. My weight had dropped by ten pounds since the last time I was weighed. I sat down while she took my blood pressure and temperature. She wrote in my chart. Once we were through with the preliminaries, I followed her to an empty room. "The doctor will be with you in a few minutes."

Dr. Fargo, a handsome elderly white gentleman, entered. He read my chart. He did a thorough examination. "I have some good news and bad news," Dr. Fargo said.

"Give me the bad news first," I stated.

He swiveled his chair around to fully face me. He handed me a short sheet of paper. I assumed it was my new prescription. "You may not need anymore anti-depressant medicine," he stated.

"I beg to differ. My life's been on a roller-coaster ride and I don't think I can cope without it," I protested.

"Parris, it may harm the baby."

"Ba-ba-by," I stuttered.

"From the symptoms you've described, it sounds like you're pregnant. We need to do some tests to make sure. I'll have my assistant call you later with your test results," he said.

My mouth flew open and wouldn't shut. I heard him talk about prenatal care but nothing was registering. I couldn't believe that I could be pregnant. I did the math in my head. It had been months since I was with Casper. My period was irregular but that's because of stress. My body always got out of sync when I had a lot on my mind.

I floated out of the office and instead of going home I went to Rodeo Drive. I went from store to store but didn't buy anything. I wandered into the baby store and found myself fantasizing about having a little boy that looked just like Casper.

"Can I help you?" one of the sales clerks asked.

I placed a toy truck back on the shelf. "No, I'm just looking."

The clerk turned her nose up. "If you're not going to buy, we do ask that you don't touch the merchandise."

I picked the truck back up. I said, "I could buy the whole store if I wanted to, but you just lost a sale because of your funky attitude."

An older woman walked up to me. "Ma'am, may I help you?"

"You can help me by hiring more courteous sales people," I responded.

"She was . . ."

I didn't wait for her to finish. I threw the truck on the shelf and heard it shatter while I walked away. A security guard who looked like he worked for the FBI came over to see what the ruckus was. He immediately recognized me. "That's Parris, Parris Mitchell," he said to the older woman.

I heard her say as I was leaving, "I don't care who she is. We have a clear policy about picking up the merchandise."

I threw my hand in the air with the middle finger visible just in case she was watching. After the incident in the store, I ended up at a French bistro. I ordered a turkey salad sandwich. The weather was nice so I sat outside and watched the cars go by as I ate. My cell phone rang off and on all day, but I didn't feel like talking to anyone. The one call I had been waiting on, never came. I guess Casper really did mean we were over when he walked out yesterday.

"You have a habit of hiding from your problems," Carmen told me over lunch the next day. She continued to lecture me about not answering my phone and how the world doesn't revolve around me. We were seated in a secluded part of the restaurant.

"Sue me," I said, as I took a bite out of my sandwich.

She clicked on her phone and listened through her earpiece. "I'll be there in an hour. Hold off sending anything before then." She turned her attention back to me. "For someone who doesn't like drama, I'm always putting out your fires."

"Good thing I have you on my team," I said in a condescending tone.

Carmen pulled out forty dollars and placed it on the table. "I got to go. I'll call you later."

Before I could respond, she was gone. I finished eating my sandwich. I pulled out a paperback novel from my purse and began to read. I wasn't ready to go home. "Is this seat taken?" I dropped my book in my plate. Casper picked it up and wiped it off. "I didn't mean to startle you."

"Sure, have a seat," I said, as my voice crackled. I took a sip of my iced tea.

I looked around because this looked like a setup. Carmen waved at me from the doorway. I ignored her.

"It's not her fault. I begged her," Casper said.

My cell phone rang. I saw the doctor's phone number displayed. I stood up. "I have to take this," I said, as I clicked the YES button and tilted my head. "This is Parris."

I listened as the physician's assistant gave me my test results. I clicked my phone off and looked into Casper's eyes and said, "You were saying?"

"What's wrong? Why are you crying?" he asked.

I didn't realize tears were falling from my eyes. I picked up the napkin and wiped my face. I wasn't prepared to share with him my news yet. "I'm fine. Just allergies," I lied.

He didn't look like he believed me, but let it drop. "It's been almost two months since we broke up." I looked around the room. He continued to say, "I've been on a roller-coaster ride but it ends today."

My heart beat slowed. I faced him. "Casper, don't do this," I said. Dealing with our breakup was hard enough. The news from the doctor and now Casper being here. I knew I wouldn't be able to control a public outburst if he said what I thought he was going to say.

Casper stood up and said, "I hadn't planned on doing this today, but you give me no choice." He reached in his pocket and pulled out the ring. The ring I left on my desk in the den almost two months prior. I assumed the maid took it and didn't care because I was so mad at him. I watched him as he bent down on one knee.

My hand automatically flew up as he took it and said, "I want you to be my wife. We've been through too much and I don't want another day to go by without you in my life. Please take me back. We can work on the trust issues. Together," he said. His eyes sparkled.

The ring sparkled. I could see people watching us. My hand shook. Time stood still. My heart wanted to say yes and I admit I have trust issues. But what if I'm right? What if he can't be trusted?

"Parris?" Casper said. "My knee's beginning to hurt, sweetheart."

I giggled. I said, "Yes. Yes, I'll marry you."

He placed the ring on my finger. While still on his knees, we kissed. We ignored the cheers going on around us. Tears flowed down both of our faces. I gathered my things and followed him outside. People congratulated us as we walked out. I ignored the clicks of phones snapping our picture.

While waiting on my car to be brought around, Casper hugged me. "I have a few errands I need to run and then I'll meet you at your place," he stated.

Still in a daze, I responded, "I'll be there."

I called Carmen on my way home. "I'm going to pay you back for that," I said, jokingly.

"You can call and thank me while you're on your honeymoon."

I chatted with her for the rest of my ride home. She was thrilled to learn we were back together. I called Mason. I got her voice mail. I hung up. What I had to tell her I didn't want left on a machine.

32

YOU AND I

I sang while I showered. I sprayed perfume over my body and put on a sexy red dress that emphasized my cleavage. "My man's coming home tonight," I sang. I danced around the room while getting dressed.

I didn't have time to cook so I called a local eatery and waited on the deliveryman. Casper walked through the door carrying the food I ordered. "I met him out front," he said.

I helped him with one of the bags. "The table's already set. Why don't you put those there?" I cleared out a spot on the table. He removed the items and we worked together to fix each other's plates.

"You've lost a lot of weight," Casper said, as he sat down.

I looked away. "Stress. I thought it was something else, but . . ." I paused for a few second. "I found out it wasn't."

"Carmen didn't tell me you were sick," he commented.

So Casper had been keeping tabs on me. I cleared my throat. "I wasn't. I had a regular checkup."

"It must have been something or else you wouldn't have said what you said."

Casper paid too much attention to what I said at times. I shouldn't complain because most women had the opposite problem with their men. I stuffed my mouth full of food and said, "I thought I was pregnant, but I wasn't."

He put his fork down. "When were you going to tell me?"

I swallowed my food. "If I was, believe me you would have been the first person to know. You weren't going to get away without taking care of your baby that's for sure."

He laughed. "I don't know if I should be sad or glad that you aren't pregnant."

"You and I both. A part of me wished that I was having your baby."

We forgot about our food as we both stood and embraced each other. "We can always get started on that right now," he said.

I playfully hit him. "Oh no, mister. You're not getting any more of this until we say 'I do.'"

"Don't make me beg for it," Casper said, right before kissing me.

We moaned as our kiss got more and more intense. I was the first to pull away. "Casper, I mean it. This time around, we're going to do this right. No sex until after we're married."

I walked away and he came behind me and picked me up. "First you torture me by breaking up with me and now this." He started tickling me.

"Enough," I said, between giggles.

Casper placed me back on the floor and said, "I

missed hearing you laugh." He planted kisses all over my face.

We spent the rest of the night talking about our hopes and fears. He became upset when I told him it was Carmen's idea to send out the press release. I felt guilty doing it after I saw his reaction. "It wasn't exactly her fault. I mean I thought you had cheated, so yes, I told her to do it," I said, hoping it wouldn't put too much of the blame on Carmen.

"She's seeing my brother. She could have gone about it another way." I could see the tension in his forehead.

I massaged his temple. "She was in agent mode and she was trying to make it easy on me."

He shook his head in disagreement. "Trevon. Did you? Did he?"

I wouldn't allow him to finish the question. "No. Trevon is just a friend. No romantic feelings on either one of our parts."

"But, he was all over you."

"That was to make you jealous, silly," I said.

He cradled me in his arms. "It worked. I had to replace the wall in the hallway."

I rubbed the muscle in the top of his arm. "Although I had broken up with you, being with another man never crossed my mind. Even when I thought you had cheated on me," I said.

Casper tightened his grip and said, "Shhh. I'm here right now. We're here together and that's all that matters."

"You and me against the world baby," I said, as I turned to face him. We kissed and held each other until we both fell asleep.

* * *

I felt his phone vibrating. He moved and answered.
I took the opportunity to go wash up. I turned and saw
Casper standing in the bathroom doorway. He looked
like he lost his best friend. "Someone ran into my
brother," he said, as I ran to hug him.

"Tell me what happened," I said, as I led him to
the bed.

"All I know is he's at Cedars. Peter called me.
They've been trying to reach me for hours."

I grabbed my keys, "Come on, I'm driving."

No one would give us any information when we got
to the hospital. I saw Carmen pacing back and forth. I
grabbed Casper's hand and led him to where she stood.
Carmen and I hugged. Her eyes were puffy from crying.

"We were driving and this car came from nowhere
and rammed into his side of the car," she said, in between tears.

Casper hugged her. "Is he okay?"

"They won't let me see him," she responded.

He rushed over to the nurse's station. "My brother's
in here. I need to see him."

The petite nurse looked like a dwarf standing next
to Casper. She said, "Sir, the doctor will be out to talk
to you shortly."

Seeing how distraught Casper was, I went to his
side and held his hand. "He's family. Can you make
this exception?" I asked in a calm voice.

She looked down the hallway. "He's in the third
room to the right. If anyone asks, don't tell them I let
you in," she said.

We turned to walk to the room. She yelled, "Only
him. You have to stay here."

I looked at Casper. "Go. I'll be right here."

I watched him rush to the room. I went and placed

my arm around Carmen. She leaned on my shoulder and cried. I patted her on the back. "Come on. He needs you. Did the police arrest the driver?"

A police officer walked up as if on cue. "Ma'am, we need to get your statement now while everything's fresh on your mind."

Normally Ms. Cool, Carmen's hands shook as she recounted the events that led up to the accident.

"The suspect is not in too good condition herself. If she comes out of it, she'll be arrested," he assured us.

Casper walked back as the conversation with the police officer was ending. "Are you related to Xavier Johnson?" the officer asked.

"I'm his brother."

"We'll need for you to give us permission to talk to him," he stated.

"He's still unconscious," Casper responded. I rubbed his back to comfort him.

The officer handed him a card. "Call us as soon as he's up to it." Before he could walk away, he turned and asked, "You don't happen to know a Sandy do you?"

Casper's fist tightened. I answered for us all and said, "Yes."

The officer walked back near us. "I hate to tell you this, but she was the driver. She's the one who hit your brother."

Casper was fuming mad. It took all of us to calm him down. I told the officer. "Are you sure the driver was Sandy Blair?"

"Yes. She said it was an accident, but we're not so sure."

I couldn't imagine what was going through Casper's mind. Sandy had wrecked havoc on our lives for so long it was surreal. Casper kept calling her every name but her birth name. "Wait until I get my hands on that trick," he said.

Carmen pulled the officer to the side and gave him more information on Sandy. The news media must have gotten wind of the story because soon after the officer left, the lobby was filling up. Carmen switched from girlfriend to agent and told the hospital security we were not to be disturbed no matter what. She agreed to have a statement to the press as soon as she could pull herself together. "We ask that you give us privacy until further notice," she wrote on a piece of paper and handed it to the nurse. She looked in the mirror and ran her hands through her hair. She walked past the security guard and I could hear the commotion of reporters.

With everything going on, I refused to watch TV or read the paper. I had more than enough of my share of media attention. "I thought you could use this," Rose said, as she and Lance walked in the waiting room with a few bags of food.

We stood up and greeted each other. "Thanks," Casper said.

Casper talked to Lance as I filled Rose in on what was going on. "If you need us to do anything, let us know," Rose said.

"Being here means a lot." I meant it. Rose, surprisingly, had become someone I could depend on. Her baby and marriage to Lance must have mellowed her.

The five of us ate, talked, and waited.

"Casper Johnson?" a doctor wearing thin-rimmed glasses asked.

Casper stood up. "How's my brother?"

"He's awake and he's asking for you." Casper looked at Carmen.

Whatever bad feeling Casper had about Carmen seemed to be erased. "Can she come to? She and my brother are really close."

I was proud of Casper. Even now, he was thinking about someone other than himself. The doctor responded, "Sure, but only for a few minutes. We think he's going to fully recover. He has a few broken ribs, but he's going to be all right."

We all let out a sigh of relief. I waited outside the room as Carmen and Casper checked on Xavier. Casper walked back out the room smiling. "He's fine. He's giving out orders."

During Xavier's stint in the hospital, he had the hospital staff eating out of the palm of his hands. If there was any doubt about Carmen and his relationship before, it was clear now they were an item. "They're letting him out of here tomorrow," she told me over the phone.

"Casper's a little upset that Xavier's staying with you and not him."

"It was his decision, not mine," Carmen said, sounding muffled.

I got his discharge time and relayed the information to Casper when he entered the room. He pulled me into his arms. "With everything that's happened, I think we need to set a date."

"Valentine's Day. That hasn't changed," I said. "I can't believe you forgot."

Casper stuttered. "I don't think I can wait that long."

"You have no choice."

33

SOLID AS A ROCK

Sandy Blair wanted to be known worldwide and she got her wish. She became a household name. Reports of her "accidentally" running into Xavier because she thought it was Casper and me in the car hit the newswire. She was charged with vehicle negligence and she lost her network job. I continued to read the article and although I should have felt bad about being happy about someone else's downfall, I didn't. There's no telling how many lives she's ruined. I closed the paper and threw it on the table. "Justice has been served," I said, as Casper rubbed my feet.

"You haven't changed your mind about going on Hailey's show have you?" he asked.

"Keep rubbing my feet or I'll name our first born Hailey."

He picked up my leg and planted kisses on my feet and worked his way up to my face. "Now, what were you saying?"

I moved him out of the way. "If we don't hurry, we're going to be late for the show."

Two hours later, we sat backstage of the *Hailey Barnes Show.* The hair and makeup stylist did their finishing touches. Hailey had Casper go on first, so he could address issues about the video and his brother's accident. I watched the monitor backstage. Others may not have noticed, but I could tell Casper was nervous, and Hailey did her best to make him feel at ease. Most of the audience empathized with his situation. Some had a few negative comments to make, but that was to be expected.

"You're on after the commercial break," the show's producer said.

Hailey showed a clip I hadn't seen before. Someone had filmed Casper's second proposal. Hailey said, "Here she is. A woman like no other. Ms. Diva herself. Parris Mitchell."

The audience stood up as I walked on the stage. I hugged Hailey and kissed Casper. We sat down. I was amazed at all of the love the audience was giving me. "Thank you," I said.

The audience applause lowered. "Congratulations on all of the awards. Your albums and singles have all gone double platinum," Hailey said.

The applause picked up again.

"Thank you. I'm blessed," I responded. The smile on my face was genuine. I was happy about Casper and me being back together and elated that my fans were cheering me on.

"The audience may recall the last time Parris was here she agreed to come back and make an announcement."

A video clip of my last appearance played. Once it finished playing, the camera zoomed in on me. Casper's arm was around my shoulders. I looked at him and placed my hand over his available hand. "Casper and I have set the date."

Hailey looked excited as she sat on the edge of her seat. "Do tell."

Casper cleared his throat and said, "We decided on February fourteenth."

"How appropriate, I'm jealous," Hailey said. She looked at her audience. "Aren't you jealous?"

We talked for a few more minutes about our upcoming nuptials. "With everything you two have been through, you deserve to be happy. It looks like their love is solid as a rock."

She did her closing commentary. We talked with the audience. Hailey talked a mile a minute as she walked us to the door. "I'm so glad you two worked things out. Girl, I thought I was going to have to do an intervention because he was sickening. Had me all depressed and I wasn't the one going through the breakup."

After we got in our waiting limousine, I said, "That's your friend."

"We're a package deal. She's your friend now too," Casper teased.

34

THE ONLY ONE
FOR ME

The next few months flew by. Between learning lines for my first acting role and Casper producing, we only saw each other every other week. It worked out because although I was the one who came up with the no more sex until our wedding night rule, my libido was on overdrive. I feigned for some Casper. Since I couldn't have him, chocolate kisses became a good substitute. I gained back ten of the pounds I lost. I went on a crash diet to lose it because otherwise I would look like a stuffed pickle in my wedding dress.

Tonight, I was hanging out with my best friend. I knew she had planned a party, but I didn't know who was invited or where it would be. My eyes were blindfolded as Carmen led me into a room. She removed the blindfold. "Surprise," people screamed.

The room was decorated with red roses. Mason and some of my sorority sisters were in attendance. "I told you I didn't want anything big," I said to Carmen as I hugged her.

My bachelorette party consisted of pampering and the attendants were all friends. Not only that, Carmen hired some male dancers to add more spice. Carmen admitted to knowing where the bachelor party was being held, so we plotted on how we would crash it. When we pulled up to Trevon's house, the bachelor party was in full swing. Twenty women got out of a couple of limousines. We convinced one limousine driver to be our front man and ring the doorbell.

I heard someone say, "I thought everybody was here." Once the door was opened, we bombarded our way in. "Surprise."

Fortunately for me, there were no strippers because I would have probably called off the wedding for good if I had seen any. Casper was sitting and talking to Xavier. He saw me and motioned for me to come to him. He stood up and hugged me. "I wondered what was taking you so long," he said.

I looked at the eye exchange between him and Xavier. Xavier stood and hugged me. "Your friend can't hold water and during one of our sessions. Well she sort of let it slip," he admitted.

Casper pulled me back into his arms. "When he told me that, I told them all to expect you ladies any minute."

Trevon and several other men handed Casper hundred dollar bills. Trevon looked at me and said, "You owe me some money."

The combined party lasted until the next day. Trevon had breakfast catered. We all left to go to our separate destinations. Casper and I spent the remainder of the day catching up on our sleep.

* * *

Between last minute fittings and making sure the wedding coordinator was on top of her job, I lost a few more pounds. With everything going on, Casper and I didn't spend much alone time together. I got a chance to meet all of his family, including a handful of his nieces and nephews and he got a chance to meet my extended family from Louisiana.

Casper's was the first voice I heard the day of our wedding. He called me on my cell phone. "Today's the day," he said.

"I'm nervous," I admitted.

"You're not having second thoughts are you?" he asked.

"I waited a lifetime for you, mister, so you're not going to get out of it that easy."

I heard him sigh. "Love you. See you on Catalina Island."

My nerves were so bad I couldn't eat. Barbara Ann said, "You don't want your stomach growling as you walk down the aisle do you?"

After a minilecture from my mom, I ate some fruit and my nerves settled.

To avoid a media frenzy, I granted exclusive access to the wedding and activities to a few reporters. Mason got her chance to be on camera. She complained at first, but after realizing she would be seen by millions, she warmed up to the idea.

I sent everyone away as I got dressed. When I walked out in the handmade imported white silk dress adorned with pearls and diamonds, Fazio marveled at me wearing his latest design. He bit his knuckle. "I've outdone myself. You look superb," he said.

The wedding coordinator sent for my mom. My mom cried and I cried. "If you don't stop, my dress is going to be ruined," I said.

Carmen and Mason walked in during our wailing session. The wedding coordinator mentioned it was time for everyone to get in place. I paced the floor. The palms of my hand were sweaty. "Do I look okay?" I kept asking my stylist.

"You look fine. But you're going to wear a hole in the carpet if you don't stop that," she said, as she reached for my hand to calm me.

The stylist placed the veil on my head. A few minutes later, my dad came through the door. "Baby girl, it's time." He held his hand out.

"Daddy, you're here," I said, shocked because he was the last person I expected to see today. I had tried to reach him unsuccessfully. After he and my mama divorced, I hardly spoke to him. He would always send me something for my birthday and occasionally called, but it had been over a year since we last spoke.

"You didn't think I was going to miss your special day did you?" he asked.

I reached for his hand and we hugged. "I'm glad you're here."

Fazio checked my dress for the last time and said, "I don't mean to break up this reunion, but it's time."

I looped my arm through my dad's as we walked down the stairway to the front of the church. The doors of the church opened to a beautiful array of red and white roses and lace shaped like bells adorned the pews. The church pews were filled with family and friends. Brian McKnight sang "The Only One for Me" as my dad walked me down the aisle. I thought my mom was going to use up all the tissue on the island as the tears flowed down her face. I didn't know if she was crying because of me or the sight of my dad. Carmen was my maid of honor and looked adorable. Xavier looked debonair as Casper's best man.

The sight of Casper standing at the end of the first pew dressed in a white tuxedo took my breath away. My father placed my hand in Casper's and we walked together to stand in front of my pastor. Although we were having our wedding on Catalina Island, I insisted it be in a church, and that my pastor perform the ceremony.

After exchanging vows, Casper and I forgot about the people who surrounded us as our kiss lingered longer than the preacher would have liked. We heard him clearing his throat. The audience laughed.

"I now introduce you to Casper and Parris Johnson."

People stood and our wedding party saluted us as we walked down the aisle as husband and wife. When we reached the outside, white doves were released into the air. We loved our family and friends, but we were eager to get away. We took the traditional wedding pictures and slipped away from the crowd behind some curtains. "I don't know if I can wait for tonight," Casper said, as he kissed me.

"I think I saw them go that way," we heard someone say.

I wiped the lipstick off his lips. "I guess we better get back," I said.

We spent about two more hours at the reception before saying our good-byes. I looked down at our hands and admired our two platinum wedding bands. With our hands entwined, we walked away from the beach and our family and friends to the waiting limousine—we were prepared to begin our new journey as husband and wife.

"I love you Parris," Casper said, as he kissed my lips

"I love you too," I replied, as my arms circled around his neck and pulled him closer.

Our lips locked as the limousine drove us to our private villa.

Double Platinum

Reading Group Guide

1. Was Parris being too hard on Casper?
2. Do you think Casper was ready to settle down when he met Parris?
3. Do you think reporters like Sandy take things overboard?
4. Casper and Hailey proclaimed to be friends. Do you think they were more than friends at some point?
5. How would you have handled running into Archie?
6. Have you or anyone you know ever taken antidepressant pills?
7. Do you think Parris was down to earth or did she have the attitude that the world revolved around her?
8. Carmen and Parris were friends as well as business associates. Would you do business with a friend and if so, do you think it would cause problems with your friendship?
9. Do you think Parris and Casper will live happily ever after? Why or why not?
10. Rose and Lance were in a previous novel, *Roses Are Thorns, Violets Are True*. How did you like their reappearance in *Double Platinum*?

ACKNOWLEDGMENTS

This book was written to celebrate my love for R & B music. My goal was to show that celebrities are people just like you and me. I've interviewed various singers and rappers and one thing I have noticed that they all have in common—they don't give up. So in spite of the obstacles that may come your way, never give up on pursuing your dreams.

Without God strengthening me when I was weak, and sustaining me through this journey, I would be lost. I'm grateful to have had two parents, Lloyd (1947-1996) and Exie Goss who showed me love and encouraged me to follow my dreams. I also have to thank my brothers Jerry and John.

This book is dedicated not only to them, but to readers and book clubs across the country and overseas who have embraced my books. Thank you!

To the memory of a friend and colleague, Katherine D. Jones. Her words of wisdom will be missed. I would like to thank everyone in the writing community for their support and encouragement over the years (too many of you all to name and I don't want to forget anyone . . . smile).

Last, but not least, a special thanks to Roy Glenn, Arvita Glenn, Carl Weber and everyone else working behind the scenes at Urban Books and Kensington Books.

Shelia M. Goss

ABOUT THE AUTHOR

Shelia M. Goss is the National Bestselling Author of *My Invisible Husband, Roses Are Thorns, Violets Are True*, and *Paige's Web*. With unique storylines, her motto is: "Bringing you stories with a twist." She was the recipient of three Shades of Romance Magazine Readers Choice Multi-Cultural Awards and honored as a Literary Diva: The Top 100 Most Admired African American Women in Literature.

Besides writing fiction, she is an entertainment writer. She's interviewed musical artists such as Mary J. Blige, India.Arie, Ne-Yo, Brian McKnight, Bow-Wow, etc. Her articles have appeared in national magazines such as *Black Romance, Caribbean Posh,* and *Jolie.* Shelia would love to hear from you. Her e-mail address is sheliagoss@aol.com or visit her Web site at http://www.sheliagoss.com or www.myspace.com/sheliagoss.